ari

The Epic Story of the Other Man

ari

Book 1

Published in the United States
by Fact & Fiction LLC

This is a work of fiction.
Similarities to real people, places, or events
are entirely coincidental.

ISBN   978-1-7362884-3-6
eBook   ISBN 978-1-7362884-1-2

Edited by Kate Seger
Interior Design by Eli Neff Akridge
Cover Design by Victorine Lieske

www.bccowling.com

Table of Contents

AFRAID OF LOVE

LOVERS WHO ONLY KISS

SILLY LESSONS

WRINKLE FREE

OF OUR OWN MAKING

NEEDING ONLY TO BE KISSED

UNFATHOMABLE

TO BLEAT OR NOT TO BLEAT

AVOIDING DISHARMONY

LOVING BEAUTY

SOBBING IN SILENCE

NYLONS & SCISSORS

ALMOST MOVING IN

APOLOGY

VISION IN WHITE

SEPARATE ROOMS OF COURSE

IT MUST STOP

ASSHOLE

I FORGOT MY HAT

THE DEAL

GO WITH LOVE

SCOTCHGUARD WORKS

BEFUDDLED

HEAD IN ASS

MAYBE THE FLU

ASK AND BE SHOWN

A CALL OF CLOSENESS

SUNDAY MOVE

WEAVING

HER SECRET

THAILAND

BLUE SUNDAY

LOST WEEK

GRIEF

CLEANSING

SHATTERED DREAMS

LOVE RUINED

SKEE BALL

LOST IN LOVE

LEARN OR DIE

THE COMFORT OF PAIN

TEARS

RETURN TO PARADISE

The cab door closed, shutting me into the backseat
Feeling cut off from love and frightened
Like a tiger cub in the wild
Hearing the steel cage snap shut
Wanting only to be back with its mother and siblings
Not knowing what separation means beyond the moment
Not knowing why

I knew we were saying good-bye
I knew why
I could see her standing on the sidewalk
Less than twenty feet away
Twenty feet and counting

The driver rocked the cab as he got in and closed his door
He slowly pulled away from the curb
Maneuvering through the traffic

I strained my neck, watching her fade away
Her image blurred by my tears
My heart ripping out from my chest
"Good-bye Beauty," I whispered
Going blind in a rainstorm of salty misery

   "Where to?" the driver asked in a gentle voice
Grateful for his sensitivity
I wanted to collapse in his arms
Into any arms
To sob openly
How could I answer this man when I could not talk?

I blew my nose

1

Still running in rebellion to life on an airplane
Running harder now with my tears
"The Ala Wai," I croaked

"Which hotel sir," he asked with such a polite tenderness
My heart opened to him
"No hotel
   My home
   I'll show you"

He asked me no more questions
As we left the airport and glided onto H-1

The Koolaus passed on my left
Those lushest of green mountains
Running almost down to the ocean on Oahu's Diamond Head side
Today holding back a white turbulence of clouds
Just waiting for a nudge to send them down over Honolulu
A nudge which seldom came

The ocean lay flat on my right
Blue and sparkling

She still stood back at the airport
Captured indelibly in my mind
The smile which lifts my heart like no other
Faded from her lips
A casualty of our situation
A casualty of our return to Paradise
From another Paradise deep in the South Pacific
Now laying hours and light-years away
Her heart as broken as mine
Her life much more confused

In pieces, I was being whisked home by my squire of the moment
In pieces, she stood still
Waiting to be collected by her husband

A man no stranger to pain

BEGINNINGS

How did I get myself in such a fix?
In love with a married woman
I, the other man
Tasting the bittersweetness
So many other women have known throughout time

The hurried hour she can snatch from a too-full life
Full of responsibilities
Duties to husband and children
Duties to today's family
Learned in yesterday's home
Watching her mother sacrifice her life for the children
Watching her father
Kind by his time and culture's standards
Yet offering no support to his wife
Caught up in his male work world
The family a loved possession
To be supported financially
Never to be nurtured from the heart

She, growing up in an Asian culture which teaches only
To keep the family together
At the expenses of personal growth.
She, having learned well
Having become the proficient wife and mother
Having been stripped of her self-confidence
Under the whip of constant criticism wielded by her older husband
Until all she could fall back upon was her illusion of harmony
Keeping peace in the home, the only goal left her
Subjugating her desires to her new family's

How did she become involved with a seeker of freedom such as
me?
A crazy impetuous creature

No stranger to illusion myself
Having looked so hard in earlier years for an escape from
discomfort
Creating more misery for myself than I could ever imagine

Always working toward freedom
No matter how circuitous the route
A never-married man of forty when I met her
Ten years younger than her husband
Knowing first-hand the attraction and pitfalls of involvement with
partially available women
Knowing and committed to a long-term struggle
To gain personal balance
To wait for the next relationship
Until strong enough to attract someone fully available
Someone committed to love and growth

We met in a neutral environment
Which allowed us to become friends
Without challenge from her husband
Without deceit upon our part
Without any intention by either of us
To bring so much pain into our lives

Looking for Spiritual love
Neither satisfied with our lives
Wanting a greater relationship with Spirit
We unlocked a puzzle box
Scrambling our divergent values
Turning our lives inside out and outside in
Leaving no moment without challenge

How more exciting can life get?
How more fulfilling?
I think I know
It is a dream I have as I write these words
A re-occurring vision

Which I can only surrender
For I have learned, I can will nothing
Except havoc

How did this start?
This adventure of love and grief

It began eighteen months before that day in April
When I left the airport in such distress
Watching her left standing alone

It began with a simple statement from a trusted friend

SCORPION'S TAIL

"Zachary, you need to learn to control your sexual energy"

It was Laureen who confronted me
Doing so with love and detachment
Surprising me completely

"That's an understatement," I said, smiling
Laying on her treatment table
Looking at the white ceiling
Thinking of the waves of hormonal assaults which had carried me
From one dance club to another the past week

The room was too cool for me

"I'm serious"
She held both my wrists
Feeling my pulses with her fingers
"You are so locked down today
    I can't get your heart open and
    I damn sure can't work on your liver flow
    Until your heart releases its blockage"

She took a deep breath
Closed her eyes and turned her attention inward

I loved Laureen deeply
She and I go back many lifetimes

Opening her eyes, she looked into mine
The light flowing around her increased
Her greenish eyes became piercing

"I guess it's time to talk about this, dear Soul," she said

7

"My sex life?"
"Yes
   No
   Dear God, I don't want to talk about your sex life"

She laughed, and her red-golden hair shook
"I want to talk about how you manage your sexual energy
   Who you do what with is your business"

She took my right hand in both of hers
Patted it gently then spoke quietly

She told me of women
Who had confided in her
Women whom she said
I had knocked off our spiritual path
With my sexual energy

She shared their feelings that I had come on to them
Then turned cold

"I haven't had sex with anyone in two years!
   How could I?"

She said she was not talking about sex
She said many women were drawn to me
That I can be a wonderful vehicle for Spirit
But a higher degree of responsibility comes with spiritual
unfoldment

She told me unless I manage myself with
Love and respect for others
I will create a great deal of negative karma for myself
"I don't want to see that," she had said

Thirty minutes later, I left
Closing the door behind me a little too hard

Not from anger but
From pain which dulled me to the outer world

The little welcome bell tinkled frantically behind me
I walked down the tiled hallway and out the back door
Feeling the warmth of Honolulu

The rest of the building was seedy
Compared to Laureen's white office
Which seemed to stay in the physical world
By the slimmest of tethers

"As you think about it
    I hope you'll understand," she had said

I thought about it
Weeding through pain and fear

"Who?"
"You know I can't tell you," she had said
Of course, I knew Laureen could not tell me
But I had to ask her, and I asked myself
Over and over again

I thought about Sandra
About Akiko
About Leslie
About Terese
About Luciane
About Ute
About Kay
About...who else?

About another Leslie, the woman at the Seminar in Florida
But Laureen would not know her
She was not even at the Florida Seminar
I knew I was wrong as I thought it

9

Laureen was where she chose to be and
Was not limited to her physical body
Like all of us
Only she had developed awareness and control
More than most

Laureen would have checked on the inner
Before bringing this up to me
She would not toss something so volatile my way on a whim

My head ached driving home
Laureen's words filling my head all evening
Before bed, I sang a Love Song to God
Singing HU quietly "HHHHUUUUU"
Watching my inner screen swirl
With the blue light of my spiritual guide

Without trying, I left my physical body
Joining my guide, Zand, on a bluff
Overlooking a vast valley of turmoil and darkness
Where all life was distraught
Just looking down into the valley
I felt heavy and drained

The HU became a strong wind roaring through me
We turned back from the cliff and
Sat on a glistening white bench washed by a pool of light
Our bodies full of tiny flashing points of light

Silently I sat by his side
Laureen's words echoing

"Is it true?" I asked
"Yes
    I've shown you the Valley
    So you will have a clear reference point

"As we unfold
    It is easy to lose sight of our growth
    Becoming careless in many ways
    Greater attention is needed
    The farther up the ladder of Spirit we climb
    It is less painful to fall from the first rung
    Than from a higher one
    And easier to start the ascent again if we have fallen only a short
way"

I felt my chair support me
The room was full of pounding blue light
The bench and the valley gone

I sat still for a long while
Still feeling the presence of Zand
Letting images flow freely through my mind

I saw Sandra's laughing face
As we crossed the street from lunch
Between our Sunday Service and
A planning meeting for our next Seminar

I joked and played with her
Sometimes risqué
Sometimes crazy
Usually throwing energy around
Energy which spun off from my frustrations
Energy I did not sit with

It was subtle
It was real
I could feel my lower chakra energy coming around from behind
Stinging Sandra with titillation and exciting outrage

Such a subtle awareness
That voicing my current thoughts

Would have brought me a hyper-sensitive label
From friends of earlier days

Now
After a few steps up the ladder, I could no longer
Stand on one foot and hang by one hand
To fool around with others nearby

I saw clearly my sexual energy
Unmanaged
Coming around to sting Sandra
Stinging Akiko
Stinging both Leslies
Stinging Terese
Stinging Luciane and Ute and Kay
Stinging who knows who else

My Scorpion's Tail
Undisciplined
Causing subtle havoc beyond my own life
Returning chaos to me
Chaos I lived but did not understand
Until now

Half the women I saw
Were still on The Path
The rest were not

The throbbing blue light in the room fell quiet

I sat alone
Feeling a sober realization
Flow into my heart

I did not want to fall
I did not want to make it difficult for others
I wanted to serve Spirit

Not do It a disservice

Like a toy pistol
Which has suddenly fired, injuring someone
I put away my Scorpion's Tail

I could not cut it off
It was part of me
But I could groom it with such a firm hand
It would not cast its sting at others

HER EYES

It was a Sunday in February
Honolulu was deep in the throes of winter
Rain every other day
Lows near sixty
Highs sometimes only into the mid-seventies
Life is tough in paradise

I sat with my back to the book display
Looking across the single room which is our Center
Watching the morning clouds dance across the crystal blue sky
No rain today

Someone passed in front of me
People were taking their seats
In the circle of chairs filling the room

I shifted my focus to the person
Who moved toward an empty seat several chairs to my right

I blinked once as my contacts blurred
Then clearly saw her
She turned and sat down in a blue chair

I stopped breathing
My solar plexus squirmed
Energy shot through me

Then I caught myself
"Stay neutral, Zak," I said aloud
Someone next to me said, "What did you say?"

I don't know if I answered
I was watching her
Thinking neutrality as my Scorpion's Tail twitched

She was Asian
She dressed simply
Expensive?
Maybe
She moved as silk cascades
Like she had been trained to wear her dignity as a protective cloak

I forced myself to look away
Then looked back immediately
She was looking at me
She smiled!
Then looked away before I could smile back
Her hair dark black?
Cut short
She wore a simple gold chain around her neck and
A beige dress

I had seen her eyes

Her high cheekbones were beautiful
The shape of her face unusual

She looked back
We both smiled at the same time
Her eyes lifted me from myself
Tossing me into the clouds

My heart raced
I calmed myself
Determined to keep my Scorpion's Tail in check

The Sunday Service started with the facilitator explaining
She would be reading a quote
From one of the books of The Path
Then we would sing HU for a few minutes
Sitting quietly in contemplation
Until she said, "May The Blessings Be"

15

She explained "HU" was an ancient name for God
Untarnished by misuse

She explained HU was a Love Song to God
Singing it was
Uplifting
Purifying
Calming and helping to bring each of us to a higher viewpoint

She told us after the HU Song and contemplation
We would break into small groups to discuss the day's topic
Then come back together near the end of the hour
To recap the discussion and end the Sunday Service

She read the quote
I did not hear it
We sang HHHHUUUUU
Then were quiet
I was barely there

We broke into small groups
The woman in the beige dress
Sat across from me in the next group
I tried not to stare
Twice our eyes met

I could not talk
I could not think
I fought to keep my stinger sheathed

I had seen her eyes and faced a major challenge

Our annual Seminar was the following weekend
I was the Director this year
In addition to coordinating the event
I had the spiritual responsibilities

16

To stay clear
To stay neutral
To be the best vehicle for Spirit I could be

At the very end of the Service
Upcoming events were announced
I was passed the microphone to discuss the Seminar

No one gasped
Shrieked or moaned
They may have laughed
I do not know
I said something
I know not what

Then she was in front of me
"Hi, I'm Ari," she said, holding out her hand
I hope I introduced myself
As I looked into her eyes, feeling her warm touch

Ever met your mother
Your brother
Your sister
Your father
Your friend
Your lover
All in one?

Past lives shot across my inner screen

She asked about the dream video showing
To be presented the following Wednesday night
She could not attend
I offered to show her the video
Whenever she had the time
I gave her my card and looked into her eyes
Again

CLEARING THE PATH

Seminar Day arrived
I managed to lose thoughts of Ari
Mulling over a hundred details

Awareness of my Scorpion's Tail
A treasured gift from Laureen

With much help from Spirit
And from my inner Guide Zand
My work through the winter
Had prepared me for this day and beyond

My stinger tucked away, I wondered if she would come
I marveled at how little real work I had to do
People old and new to The Path and each other
Set up the one-day seminar at the University School of Travel
Working fluidly
Smiling with love and joy

Then she was there
Late in the morning
After I had bumbled my Introduction to the Seminar

We talked
Went to the same workshop on dreams
I asked her to have lunch
She said, "Yes"...!

I drove her to a corner market
My sandwich chicken and feta
Hers a garden burger

We talked and laughed
She wore a gentle restraint

Not like the women I am usually attracted to
Half-wild, uninhibited in their expression
Of who they are
Of what they feel

I felt a warm closedness about her
Yet a tremendous attraction hung between us
She had my attention as no woman had ever

Spirit flowed so strongly
I had no problem with my Scorpion's Tail
It laying quiet well-trained and
Soothed by the steady flow of spiritual energy

I looked into her eyes
Found rivers of shared past experiences but
Remained very quiet about them

The realization I was to clear the path for her
Settled over me in a taffeta cloak of golden light
I saw my job was to make her initial steps on The Path
Free of unnecessary clutter
Without pulling her

If a person on The Path tries to influence another
They don't do it for long
It is foolish to interfere in another's choice
When the price paid
Is so clear quick and increasingly severe

If she wanted to walk The Path
I could walk with her
I could clear away any boulders Spirit directed me to move out of
her way

She told me she was married
Had two girls

Sarah and Sally
Ten and eight
She was Thai
Her husband Swedish
I suggested her kids were "Sweets"
She laughed with reserve

She said she had a happy marriage
I did not believe her but
Stayed neutral

She asked if joining The Path
Meant having to give up her lifestyle
Her home
Her things
Her family

I said, "No
    There are no rules which require anything like that"

What went unspoken
Was the experience of thousands before her who walk The Path
With each step
Spirit enters our lives more fully
Bringing greater awareness

It's not possible
To live with Spirit more each day
And remain asleep

Whether she would face losing her home or family
Would depend on the sum of all her past choices
In her past lives and
How well she listened to her inner voice
And her inner guides

If she went far enough on The Path she would have to give up

Her attachment for everything or possibly have it taken away

I did not mention this irony of surrender to Spirit
Of giving up everything
Yet being given all we need
More than we can imagine
As long as we do not become attached

Only she could answer her questions and
She did not know this
Yet

I knew I would do anything to help her
That I must do everything I could
To prevent her from facing the choice
Between her husband and The Path

OPENING TO SPIRIT

The Seminar ended
I continued writing a short story, which grew
Into the "B-" word
Book

I finally said it
"I'm writing a book"
After spontaneously buying a used laptop
Overpriced but owner financed
To take with me to the Springtime International Seminar in DC
For those studying—or interested in—The Path

I wrote every day home and away
Thanks to the new computer
Ignoring work
No longer an independent loan officer
Now scrambling hard as Vice-President
To push our business to a new level
Had resulted in good cash-flow
For the early months of the year

Ours a very small company
The new underwriter we hired
On one hundred percent commission like Bob and I
Offered her perspective
When we told her she would also be Vice-President
"Vice-President of Nothing" she confided to the one person not
on commission
Our "Comptroller" from mainland China
A finished thesis away from an MBA in business
With a bent for working madly on a project
Without bothering to ask for directions
Unaware he did not know what he was doing in crucial areas

Wonderful guy
So willing to help
An engineering degree from a society which discourages
competency
Discourages personal initiative
Lost at sea in a small business
Where everyone must do everything
With a minimum of guidance

I was Senior VP of Nothing
Not caring
Wrapped up in writing
Living off my recent efforts
I showed up most days
Took out the trash as needed
Created the illusion I was working
When I was thinking about the book instead
Thinking about Ari

She called often
She invited me out for an evening occasionally
She sent me a birthday card in April
When she was off island
Inside a single ticket to a Mozart Concert
And a note saying
She was sorry she could not go with me
Thanking me "For always being there"

I was touched deeply
Wondering what I had done
To always be there for her

Carefully so very carefully our friendship unfolded
A brief hug and a kiss on the cheek
Limited discussion about her marriage
No Scorpion's Tail stinging
No subtle desires pushing to the surface

Our friendship richening

The deep bond was there
She was never far from my attention
But always pushed down just below the surface
Listening to Spirit to know what to do next
To clear The Path for her

She acted married not joining us for lunch
After Sunday Service

She acted married
Often ending a phone conversation
With abrupt reference to "him"

"He's coming
    He wants me to watch a movie with him
    He's calling to me from the top of the stairs"

"I better go
    He wants
    He demands
    I have to please him"
Was the unspoken message
I wondered what kind of marriage she had
Calling her husband "he" and "him" without affection
Without revealing the desire of being together

She acted married
But she did not feel married
Not in the true sense

I said nothing
We talked about spiritual principles
About the steps she was taking along The Path

Two years of study are required

Before someone can elect to walk The Path
Stepping off is always possible
But easier if done in the first two years

Some people race ahead
Overdosing on Spirit
Burning off too much karma in too short a time
Their lives temporarily a wreck

Some people are more steady

Ari was feeling her way by the inch
Coming from a culture which taught her
To subvert her feelings and desires
To serve her parents
To serve her husband
Making spiritual liberation a step into the unknown

Yet she took the steps
Drawn by the Light
Drawn by the Sound
The inner Light and Sound of God
Which is everywhere for everyone
Waiting to be recognized
By those willing to risk opening to Spirit

SEXUAL CHAOS

No subtle desires pushing to the surface
In my friendship with Ari
Complete control of my Scorpion's Tail
In all matters pertaining to The Path

In the rest of my life
Sexual chaos
My stinger leading me

Leading the pull between hormones and survival
In a world changed by AIDS

Spiritual awareness had changed my world
I knew I could not limit matters pertaining to The Path
To the time spent at the Center
Spiritual unfolding involves all of life

I kept my chaos hidden
Pushed back and down
Away from my friends
From other people on The Path
From Ari
But I was running amok

Leaving HU Songs
Going straight to dance clubs
Asking any women who smiled at me for more
None agreed thankfully
They were doing their job
Enticing me
Not wanting to be away from their work
With a balding forty-year-old
So captured by his need and Aries directness
He was not capable of delaying gratification long enough

27

To meet a woman under more natural circumstances

I got shot through with titillation
Sating my habit begun twenty years earlier
In the dance clubs and porn movie house of Indiana
A youth reaching out for love
Without the ability or good sense
To look beyond the moment
Beyond his childhood pain of abandonment

DANCING WITH A TREASURE

Our local Center gave a dance at the bandstand in Kapiolani Park
Inviting anyone interested to come
Dance in the Light and Sound

Fifties music
Sixties music
A couple of Virginia Reels and the Hokey Pokey

I sat silently off to one side
Watching the others dance
Obeying Laureen's orders earlier in the day to get some rest
Exhausted from too much writing
Too much creative flow
Testosterone poisoning and too little sleep
Laureen had admonished me
For having run down my body
The lowest she had seen me in two years

I promised to be good

I was good
Until I saw Ari and her girls
Walk into the pool of floodlights surrounding the bandstand

In a moment I was by her side
Laughing
Playing with the girls
With them for only the second time

Sally swiped one of my shoes
Whooping I chased her
She fled squealing

Then Sarah had my other shoe

I ran and ran
Catching them
Letting them go
Not being able to catch them
Stopping to talk with Ari
She and I pushed onto the dance floor by the girls
As a couple

Dancing slowly with Ari
Holding her like a priceless treasure
I was not sure was mine to hold

We all did the Hokey Pokey
The girls, Ari and me bumping into each other
As comfortable as puppies

I noticed Laureen near the edge
Moving closer to her
I yelled, "Just following doctor's orders"
She smiled
Lighting up the dance floor even more
"I can see
    I can see"

Then it was over
The music was done
People milled around
Sally brought us cups of punch

The girls ran out into the park benches
Playing some game
Among the seats used for watching performances
They discovered a homeless person sleeping in the back row

Then their father was at the very edge of the light
The girls ran to him
Telling him all about the dance

He had with him the teenage daughter of a friend
Whom the family was going to take to the airport
For a midnight flight home

I hung back from Ari as she joined her family
Until she motioned me forward

As I stepped into the group
I saw her husband's face for the first time
"Zak this is Robert
    And our friend's daughter Kelly
    She's on her way back to Taiwan"

Robert and I shook hands
I was stunned
He was older than Ari
Much older with a heavily lined face
A slight, almost weak physical presence
Not someone I would picture her with

Later I wondered if it had been the light
Or lack of light
Which had cast him in such an unappealing shadow

After they left I bounced as I walked home
Heart light from our touching as we danced
With a growing emptiness
Missing her sparkling company

I guided myself back to clarity
Bringing my role in her life back into sharp focus

MOMENT TO MOMENT

Spring bled into summer
I wrestled with my hormones
Ari stopped by the office
Sometimes we had lunch

Her experience with the HU
With the inner Light and Sound
Deepened
Our friendship
Also deepened without an extra word of acknowledgment

Time for the Summertime Seminar in Anaheim arrived
She was not sure until the last minute
She was going

Anyone's first major Seminar is an event
Even if they sail through it
Oblivious to their inner changes

Singing HU with five thousand people
Listening to Sri Thomas the spiritual leader of The Path
The Outer Master currently available for inner guidance
Available to any who asked
Who also runs a full-time physical body
Subject to the same lower world Passions of the Mind
We all are

His stories are special
Weaving their meanings on many different levels
Full of humor and love
Stories of everyday events
Looked at with an eye toward uncovering Spirit's hand
In all life

Not bound by full-time physical bodies
Already having spent their time suffering and growing in the
physical
Other Masters remain available in the inner worlds
To all who are open to them
Manifesting in the physical when needed
But less able to bridge the inner and outer
As effectively as a Master who runs a physical body 24/7

I went early for the Writer's Conference
Preceding the Seminar in Anaheim
Then Ari was at my hotel room door
Knocking
Beauty
Whom I dared not call so
She had arrived an hour earlier
Coming to see her good friend

I pushed away my desire for her
And romped through the next two days
With Beauty
With Joe
With Henri
With Diane and her very fresh baby
With the adorable blue vein
Atop its little head
About which Joe wrote a song
To the tune of "Amazing Grace"
And sang as a love song
"Amazing vein on top my head
    That's blue and bulging out
    Someday my hair will grow so long
    No one will find out"

Saturday I met two women
One of whom interested me
But not yet

33

The other captured my stinger with her own sexual snare

She made her living doing strip-a-grams
I followed her around shamelessly as soon as I picked up her scent
With Ari, Joe, and Henri in tow

Late in the night I was alone in my room with both women
Watching a movie
Cruising on the amazing high energy of the Seminar

The not-yet-of-interest woman left in the middle of the night
The other woman
With the compelling sexual energy and questioning openness
Which drew me as strongly as her scent
Stayed what was left of the night
We almost made love in the morning
But a distant voice finally pierced my obsession
Telling me to pass her by

I dressed in a haze of exhaustion
Leaving her sliding back into sleep
To rush to the early Sunday morning HU Song
The special one

Throughout the seminar Ari had saved me seats
For different programs
While I volunteered
Setting up and tearing down workshop rooms

As I rushed to the auditorium that Sunday morning
I knew I had lost something
But I did not know what

I found Joe and Ari together near the front
They had not saved me a seat
They had not known if I would be coming

I was desolate knowing I had created my isolation

A seat in front of Ari opened up just before the HU began
I thanked Spirit for the gift
For sparing me from being sent to the back of the auditorium
Away from her

Much later in our friendship
I learned that she really did not mind
That I was with the woman with the sexual snare
She just did not like her much

I did not like leaving Ari
I learned that Sunday morning in Anaheim
I needed to be by her side
Listening to her
Listening to Spirit
Surrendering my needs
Surrendering my passions
Whatever was building
Whatever the form our friendship was too take

It is a buoyant, exhilarating feeling
To set aside personal needs for someone
A decision I made without hesitation

Living it moment to moment is the test
My test

MY LOCAL EDITOR

Ari was gone for July
To Europe for the family's summer visit
To the homeland of her husband's father
With his quick smile
His sharp tongue
His closed heart
As she described him

I missed her
But did not dwell on it
She was gone
She was married
She was my friend

I finished the second rewrite
Of my B-Book
Sent it to an agent in Pittsburgh
Who responded promptly
With a request for eighteen hundred dollars for editing

Thanks but no thanks
I looked around Honolulu for a local editor

In the health food store
In my way
As I headed for the door with work on my mind
Stood Gwen

A woman on a motorcycle I had met in April
Letting her spend one night on my floor on my folding futon pad
Because she was tired and
Did not to want to ride back to the north shore
On her Honda 150
Only to return in the morning

To give three piano lessons

It was a strange evening
Gwen's soft core hidden under her hard surface
Studded with rigid opinions
Seeking power powerlessly
Shutting herself off from Spirit
Making her path so much more difficult than seemed necessary

But who can really tell
Where another is with Spirit?
The more I learn about myself the more I see
I am doing exactly what I need to be doing in that moment
Even if it is not my best
I am still learning
Still unfolding

It must be that way with everyone
Whether they can express it or not

Standing in the health food store doorway
Gwen and I exchanged one sentences summaries of our lives
She was between official homes
Living with friends
Living out of a storage locker
Frantic and kinetic
Appealing in a way

My writing
My experience with the Pittsburgh agent
Came tumbling out

Gwen reminded me
She was a "crack" editor with east coast training
I did not question her self-appraisal

We agreed to meet the next evening

To discuss working together

I had feelings in many directions
But let them go
Willing to watch this adventure unfold

We did meet almost as planned
Gwen was twenty minutes late

"Whimsical out-of-body adventures
    Nearly hidden spiritual principles
    A madcap tour through a zany world"

Gwen grew more interested in my manuscript as I described it
Reminding me books are books only upon publication
Manuscripts until publication
The same way writers become authors

Too picky for my broad strokes
But I needed input
Sorting it out a job for later

We went to my office to draft a short contract
Amid a mutual hunger

Mine for feedback
Hers for money and recognition

The small negotiations became sticky
We barely agreed on her earnings
Should the work get published with her changes intact
We agreed that she would first do a line-by-line review
Then an overview

I gave her the first payment
Against the nudge of my inner voice

We had our first meeting a week later
The two hundred pages she promised were half done
Her line-by-line comments crisp

Some disagreement
Some clarification
Lots of her opinions
Divergent attitudes

She liked my viewpoint
Begrudgingly

I reworked the first hundred pages
At our next meeting she had little done
I gave her my rewrite
We talked too much
I left determined to practice the law of silence in the future

Some people invited sharing
With their open readiness
When my ego kicks in I trip over my human consciousness
Forgetting to listen to Spirit's direction

Gwen's brick-hard stack of opinions inviting quixotic flailing
As useless to me as her

Her editing I liked so we continued
Next week
Next meeting
Some more work done
Another payment
The manuscript was reforming
She liked my rewrite

She called me sooner than agreed
Needing the balance of her fee
To move in that night with a woman she said

Would be a perfect roommate for her
The nest she had been longing for
In town, near many of her piano students

I gave in
She was at her appealing best promising me
When all her agreed upon work would be done
Until I felt callow for asking
Giving her word freely

I also had another nudge from my inner
"Mistake" It said

The roommate was ideal for less than a day
By the weekend Gwen was house sitting
For an off-island friend
About whom Gwen had little good to say

No work from her
Life too stressful
More promises
Two weeks later she showed up in my driveway
Raging at the traffic

Raging as though she had been forced
To marry a republican businessman
For her something to truly rage about
Traffic a convenient scapegoat

I tried to sooth her
She escalated
Quickly I reached my limit
Told her to come back when she was sane
Closing the door behind me
To keep her outside
She left
With the last hundred pages of the rewrite

No phone calls returned
Her friend back from her trip
With nothing good to say about Gwen
Telling me Gwen was living with her sometimes boyfriend

I called
He was pleasant
No response from Gwen

I let it go after complaining to anyone who would listen
And finished the rewrite myself

Her input was valuable
Worth the full fee
Even though less than half our contract was fulfilled

Sometimes I handle people with the energy they throw at me
Mixing it with my own discomforts
Satisfying my in-the-moment urge
Creating incomplete exchanges

The experiences with my local editor were mine to digest
I had a book to sell

WANTING DESPERATELY

A third round of query packages sent out
Thirty-plus carefully researched small presses this time
A rewritten query letter
Summary, chapter synopsis and sample chapter

Before the early return of rejection letters
Could cross in the mail with the stragglers
From the two previous mailings to agents
I asked Ari out to a movie

She asked Robert who said "yes" without any voiced concern
We kidded and laughed about our "date"

A night-out
Including celebrating Ari was going to the World Wide
The next major Seminar on the mainland
The first in St. Louis
Where we could visit the just finished Temple

A night-out
Which ended on the beach under a blooming moon
Hand-in-hand walking in silence
Treasured friendship running deep

The night out was a calming oasis
A time-out from the rush of work
From the push to complete the mailing
From my daily struggle with hormonal overload

My many-edged sword of intimacy
Too convoluted to dissect
Too powerful to turn away
I hung on trying to survive my attempts at chronic self-destruction
Seeking love where it was not

My Scorpion's Tail in firm check with Ari
With other women in my work world
With other women on The Path
But let loose like a maverick wildebeest during other moments

I was trying desperately to stay away from the dance clubs
Whenever I spent money there it seemed to dry up at work
The Law of Economy can be exacting when abused

Amid this blurred autumn
A subtle event in Honolulu
I picked up a copy of the Buy and Sell island newspaper
Filled with cars, computers and junk for sale

Under Personals were several ads for dating services
I was sure they were less than legitimate
But decided to call anyway
Just to see

Later at home on that Saturday afternoon
I dialed
Three were dull
Obviously referral services
Where "date" began with "How much"
Not of conscious interest but my imagination was awakened

I called another
Sex dripped from the receiver
Fun for thirty seconds
Too strong to pursue

The last add read
"Hawaii's Finest"
A pleasant man answered
Asking discreetly what sort of woman I might be interested in

My hormones now throbbing
I pushed aside the dim memories
Of a previous latex-coated experience
With women choosing money over love
Perhaps they like I had slipped into a groove
Which held no love

Such a fruitless dance
Looking for love outside of ourselves
Yet so necessary a step in learning about love
About Divine Love

Divine Love was far from my mind as the phone rang
Jasmine as promised

She sounded so sweet and willing
I did not ask anything outrageous
I even asked that if we liked each other
Could future time together perhaps include dinner first

"Of course" she said softly purring into my ear

Unfortunately she was leaving soon for the Big Island
We set a tentative date for Tuesday evening

Primed for instant gratification
But now having to live with the decision until Tuesday
Knowing Spirit was giving me time to reconsider

Wanting the experience desperately
I pushed aside any inner warnings
Focusing only on Tuesday evening
Focusing on satisfying my needs

I worked little Tuesday afternoon
Did not eat
Bought a new bottle of massage oil

The old one mostly used for safe sex for the single man
Bought an assortment of condoms

Tuesday at seven o'clock I called the contact number
Told the pleasant voice of my agreement with Jasmine
She called back in minutes

"Nine o'clock"
Would that work for me she wanted to know
"Of course"

The hotel I was to visit was just down the block
Was nicer than made sense
For someone charging such a reasonable rate

I bounced around my apartment
On the sharp needle-point of expectation

On the short walk to the hotel Spirit nagged softly
Testing me to see how much I wanted this experience
I wanted it badly

I walked by the Honolulu Police Department three-wheeler
Sitting near the open lobby
Cops are everywhere in Waikiki

I walked by a herd of families
Waiting for the buses to come shuttle them to an evening luau
Or the Polynesian Cultural Center
Waiting for their Hawaii experience

The elevator opened on the sixth floor
The hallway slightly damp and mildewy
Unlike the breezy lobby
The room was five doors away
I knocked
The door was opened by a beautiful local hapa woman

Half Asian, half not
She invited me in

She did not have on the short skirt I had requested
At her asking "What would you like me to wear?"
She was dressed casually not provocatively
Jeans shirt and a vest
I wondered about the vest

Her eyes soothed my questions
She asked again what I wanted to do
I told her
She repeated my request
Changing my words to more exact almost clinical ones
She asked if I had the money
I gave her a thin stack of twenties

She said she would be just a moment and went into the bedroom
I watched her go to the closet
To change and tuck-away the money I assumed

No

Suddenly two football players jumped into the room
One from behind the curtain near me
One from the bedroom brushing by the hapa woman

I was under arrest for soliciting a prostitute

FUDGE SUNDAE PARTY

The handcuffs closed around my wrists cold and tight
I kept replaying the scene
Watching where I could have stepped aside
Avoiding what I now faced

The woman stayed out of sight in the bedroom
The football players were humorless
Searching my pockets
Somehow overlooking my business cards
"Occupation" one asked
"Writer" I answered
Not wanting to drag our company into the papers
Thankful that there was nothing on me
Connecting me to The Path
I would have to resign as Local Director
Wondering if I would be banished
No I decided
There are no witch hunts on The Path
Every step along The Path made possible by experience
I might be asked to step down from my leadership position
Maybe not
As informal as the organizational structure is
Maybe not
I would ask Ethel our Hawaii Director
And offer to resign

More questions from the goons met with basic answers
Hoping they would just me let go

"I was just horny" I said whining
"We all get horny" one of them replied still busy with his paper work
"But you broke the law"

Wondering if I had been wronged
Wondering if I had to follow laws that are unfair

I was squirming big time in the physical and my inner bodies
Feeling like an animal about to be sacrificed
Wanting to avoid the experience facing me
Standing directly in my path

I sang HHHHUUUUU silently
Felt the calming cloak of Spirit fall over me
Showing me right and wrong are not the issue
I chose this action
I live the outcome

I chose to live in this society
As Soul choosing Its situation to be born into
To best work on issues needed to master

As my adult human consciousness
Free to live in another country
If I did not like the rules of this one
I had chosen to live in Honolulu and
In doing so agreed to live by the rules of this society

I had read about the crackdown
The tougher prostitution law enacted in the summer
I had ignored Spirit's nudges
Now I was about to live the experience I had asked for so loudly
It just was not what I expected
Or wanted

My denial surged when I was taken down to the lobby
One of the goons carrying my little bag
Of massage oil and condoms

I was forced to wait in the open lobby
Sitting on my handcuffed hands

The herds of families there when I came in
Thankfully gone

A white squad car came
The back seat was barren and grey with little leg room
The handcuffs cut into my wrists

I felt so helpless
So angry with myself

The ride downtown was brief
The police station located on Young Street
Two miles short of downtown
I parked nearby whenever I saw Laureen for a treatment

Thoughts of what would happen
Ended when the car door opened
Wiped out by the events themselves

I was walked into a basement room
Logged in
Locked into a cell to wait
Then fingerprinted
Photographed front and side

These cops were nearly human
Joking with each other like jocks
Slightly warm
Slightly tolerant of me

I was told I could get out with five hundred dollars bail
I had sixty bucks
Could not use the evidence
The slim stack of twenties
Given to the vanishing hapa woman
Far from enough anyway

The vanishing woman appeared
Sliding into the station looking uneasy
"Tracie's bust" someone said
They cheered
I was her trophy

I was told I could make a phone call
Who to call?
I thought of Ari immediately
Spirit yelled "No"
I did not want her husband to know
Someone on The Path had been busted
Her friend in jail
My inner said this would come back to her
He would use it at some point making her way harder

Laureen
I reached for my wallet
My card with friends' numbers on it
The police had it
I had to ask someone to get it for me
Small hassle
Then the wallet was in my hands
I dialed Laureen's number
Busy
My heart slipped
I took several deep breaths
Felt pressured to make my call
The cop standing next to me
Waiting to get back to his whatever

I called again
Her son answered
"See if I can call him back"
She asked him from the background
I said it was important

A moment later she was on the phone
"What's the matter Zak?"
I told her why and how and where I was
What I needed
"We'll be right down. How much?"

I was locked into a worse than barren cell
A holding tank I think it was called
No seats
Part of the wall jutting forward forming a low concrete bench
So people
Prisoners
Would not have to sit on the floor
The cell painted with coats of depression
A stark urinal by the door
Shielded only slightly from the room of cops

My heart beating a thousand times as each moment passed

Then someone arrived in my line of vision
My name was called
Laureen and Ernie were there

More moments full of hours
Court papers stuffed into my hands

Then I was in both their arms
So grateful
So humiliated
So angry with myself

They welcomed me with love and laughter
They were laughing!

Laughing at all the experiences Soul must go through
Laughing because they love me without judgment
Love me as Soul

I felt like I was coming home to a Fudge Sundae party
After breaking the neighbor's window

Expecting the stern reprimands of an old consciousness
Finding the fluid acceptance of Divine Love instead

They ask if I wanted to go somewhere and talk

"Yes – No" I did not know
Then I knew I must go home

The clock said ten before eleven
When I stepped into my apartment
Home less than two hours
Since my "date" with Jasmine

I laid down
My heart throbbing in fear
So keenly aware of what I had chosen
Over staying home writing
Sixty pages into a new book
Flowing well
Knowing my work rhythm was now blown and
Hoping I could pick it up again

I HUed again
Felt Spirit keenly
Knowing I had been given the experience I needed
As smoothly and painlessly as possible

Grateful
I reached for the phone to share my experience with Ari
Not sure how she might receive it

FIRST LIGHT

Ari was more than supportive
She would have come willingly if I had called she said
So glad I did not call her
So glad that this garbage of mine was not spilled at her feet

She told me she wished she could help me with this problem I was
stunned
What did she say?

Did she say she wanted to make love with me?
Or did she mean
Simply to "help" with a problem

So unlike her to infer any possible physical relationship
No matter how remote
The first time
She let any light pass under the door of sexuality between us

I let her statement stand
Cherishing her friendship
My stinger in solitary

Two weeks later
The weekend of the World Wide arrived
My recent trouble
Still numbing my consciousness

A LINK

A Golden source of Wisdom here on Earth
A place of amazing harmony and Spiritual openness
Shaped out of rolling hills southwest of St. Louis
The Temple was said to be gorgeous

Built by many people of many spiritual paths
All seeing it as a special building
Created to provide a tangible link
Between the inner worlds of pure Spirit
And the outer worlds of the physical
Where Spirit struggles to manifest
Built for those who can make use of such a link

Soon after checking into my hotel room Thursday late morning
She knocked on my door
So good to see her
She sat on my bed tentatively
Talked of the clean feeling she had coming to this city

Relaxed as I had never seen her relax
She had asked questions about
Spirit
Soul
Karma
Why did I have to go through what I go through?
What will she have to go through?
Why does growing hurt?
"It doesn't always" I said grinning

Then we were out of the room
Our hearts lingering
Forbidden words unspoken
Lunch and the Temple calling to us

54

Ari and I rode to the Temple in a bus full of happy people
Many from Hawaii
Sitting together
Feeling like a couple but acting like friends

As the bus rounded a bend and crested a small rise
Forty minutes from the downtown area
A flash of gold struck me
Then we all saw the golden ziggurat roof of the Temple
Built to symbolize Soul's movement
From the lower worlds of human conscious
To the higher worlds of pure Spirit

Cool St. Louis fall air
Greeted everyone
Those from Hawaii bundled more than most
I freezing
Trying to detach from fears of illness and let Spirit shield me

The Temple stood low and graceful
On the many acres surrounding it
Golden-hued stone and concrete columns and walls
Locked together
Two octagons
Three squares forming
Sanctuary
Vestibule and administration area

Barely in the physical
A link between Inner and Outer

Ari and I walked hand-in-hand
Until she became self-conscious

A large luminescent blue star hung over the sanctuary
An outer manifestation
Of so many people's inner experience

The Blue Star
One inner sign of the presence of the Inner Guide
The guiding consciousness
Passed from Spiritual Leader to Spiritual Leader
Working with both the Light and Sound of God
By any name
Throughout time

FARTHER THAN I COULD SEE

The weekend Seminar passed by in a blur of
Talks
Workshops
Friends
Dinner
All with Ari

We were together day and evening
Parting reluctantly late each night
She firm in her conviction
Her marriage gave her all she needed in a relationship

I knew her words
If not hollow
Were less than full
I did not probe

She welcomed my touch
An affectionate friend

She purred
When I massaged her on my bed
Fully clothed

She agreed
When I said we were platonic lovers
Walking down a flight of stairs
Then turned suddenly saying "No"

Truth and reality
Struggling to coexist

She said "Watch it Buster"
When I made a playful proposition

Late one evening in the elevator going to her room
Effective when she left her husband

For a moment I wondered if I had offended her
Then she was bright with smiles

Glowing throughout the weekend
Feeling the incredible flow of Spiritual Love
Present at all major seminars of The Path
She was more open now than in Anaheim
Bathed by the Light
Resonating with the Sound

Walking back from her hotel Sunday night
Through spitting snow
Through my fear of the cold
Through the middle of a Minnesota Twins World Series
celebration
Spilling incongruently out of a St. Louis sports bar
I walked through the heart of my love for Ari
Seeing it
Undeniable and whole for the first time

I had said to a friend the day before without thinking
The words rolling out like someone whispered them into my ear
"She's married
     But I can't imagine her being married
     To the same man at least
     Five years from now"

Walking home I saw the months behind us
Shining with a special light
And the time ahead of us stretching out farther than I could see
Even with my inner vision

MY OWN SEWER

After St. Louis Ari and I spent more time together
Friday evenings twice a month after Laureen's class
We walked on the beach talking
Being quiet and close
After Sunday Service
Trips to the park
Or a museum
And occasionally an evening in each other's company

I skirted the edge of a nasty flu
Lungs heavy

I tried to prepare myself for court

I learned about pleading a deferred acceptance of guilt
Which could be erased in the future
Scrubbed from my record if no other trouble appeared

I felt better with this knowledge
But far from clear
Heard the fine could be a thousand dollars
Scary with cash flow low
Business sluggish
Good loans dragging without apparent explanation
Though I knew why

Laureen and Ernie only partially paid back
I day-dreamed of changing any one of a dozen decisions
Leading up to being busted
Any of which would have saved me the pain and humiliation

I knew the experience was a loud alarm from Spirit
A shout to discipline this part of me
Its voice lifted

Over-riding the clamor of my obsession
An opportunity to cleanse
A demand for payment from so many past choices made
Despite ongoing inner warnings

A Tuesday morning downtown in District Court
Too much air conditioning
Seeing one of the football player goons in a suit
Slip through the door next to the courtroom
Ready to testify

The Judge
A no-nonsense woman with a crisp sense of fairness
Explaining to all the options
Going into great detail about deferred acceptance of guilt

I felt lighter hearing her words

I looked around for TV cameras or reporters
Saw none

I watched people file before the bench
Explaining why they were there
Some dealing with their problems
Some postponing

Street girls from the night before
The men who drank too much
The ones who fought with each other
And themselves

Women who did not speak English
Perhaps only for the day

Several cases of people who had failed to get auto insurance
A serious affair in Hawaii

Then I was the only one left
Called before the Judge
Feeling very naked
Eternally grateful no one was scribbling
For tomorrow's paper

Charges read
How did I plead?
I asked for a deferred acceptance of guilt
Thinking I was polite in asking

The Judge mumbled something incoherent
Looked through a book in front of her
Then said she could not grant me a deferred acceptance
Since the law had been changed that July
Full sentencing was mandatory
The prosecutor—also a woman—agreed

Standing under a hidden spotlight
Two women holding the strings
I pleaded guilty accepting the permanent record
Grateful to hear the fine was only my five hundred dollar bail

I left the courthouse to a sunny Tuesday morning
Relieved but quickly sinking into depression and anger

I talked to a woman at the street corner
Who spoke in half-hidden phrases
Then walked two blocks with her toward Chinatown
Before realizing she had also just been in court
Busted the night before for being on the streets
Too long on one corner
Talking to too many men

For a moment I was intrigued
Then shook myself out of it

My feet pounding pavement
I walked around downtown
Anger and libido mixing
Seeking release from the pressure
Saw a woman in tight jeans and cowboy jacket
Cross the street in front of me
I complimented her jacket awkwardly
Insincerely

She was civil
Just
Appeared to be meandering
I thought about propositioning her but
Feared rejection
Feared acceptance
Feared my own self-destructive energy

I broke away from her
Found my car and drove home
Went to work
Did not work much
Walked up and down Ala Moana Center's half-mile of multi-level
mall
Looking at women's crotches
Rage hammering

Went to a nearby dance bar
Looked at women's crotches
Without needing imagination

Ask a dancer out for dinner
She took my card

Went home again feeling helpless
Caught in my own sewer

Laid on my bed for hours

Wanting to cry
Wanting to see Ari
Feeling low and worthless

Feeling far away from my writing
Which had stopped with my arrest
Wondering if I would ever get passed my own hormones
Ever learn to manage my creative energy

TIME TO LEAVE

Ari told me casually one day
Sally's birthday was coming up

"Isn't that when Robert will be in Europe?"
"Yes"
"Has he done something special
    to make up for missing his daughter's birthday?" I asked
"No" she said
"He has been gone for her birthday several times before
    I don't think he has gotten her anything
    Maybe when he returns"

I was appalled
A girl turns nine and her daddy has to be away
But treats it like just another day

I shut down my judgment
Knowing it would only come back to me

Two days later with Ari
While looking for a toy cash register for my nephew
I saw a box of face-paints

The next day I bought them and
Sent them home with Ari after our class
For Sally's birthday

I had only met the girls a few times
At restaurants mostly
Yet knew them well through Ari's deep love for them

When my nieces were eleven and nine
As were Sarah and Sally by now
I spent wonderful times with them

Playing and fighting
Showing them Minneapolis
Letting them be little adults for a week a few times a year

Our lives have flowed differently the past seven years
Seeing them little

My heart's place for Sarah and Sally already made
With longing just below the surface

I was invited to dinner the day after Sally's birthday
The paints had been a hit
"Fun" Ari told me they said

I showed up early and eager
Then found the energy did not flow as easily with them
As it did in my mind
I had overlooked getting to know two people

But in moments we were romping and squealing

With puppy dogs and kids
The floor is always the best playground

After dinner we played nine-year-old word games
Then the paints came out
Soon we four had masks of swirls and dots
Ari making splendid designs on her halves of both girls faces
My strokes clumsy everyone agreed

We took pictures
All combinations
Tongues out
Carnations behind our ears
On the love seat
Between Ari and Sarah
My arms around them both

Sally directing us into absurd poses

Family energy overwhelmed me
Seductive
Yet not my family

Later in the evening after goodnight hugs from the girls
Ari and I laid on pillows on the floor
Listening to Mozart's requiem

Our bodies seemed drawn together
Each move made by one echoed by the other like lovers in bed

Time to leave

LEAVING FOR BALI

"I need you" came running out of my mouth
Before I could think about what I was saying
About how she might feel
About anything

We sat in her car after Sunday Services at the Center
About to part for the last time
Before her flight to Bali the next morning
Now we sat in silence

Our only conversation my cough from the flu
I had outrun until I could run no further
Caught in a frenzy of my own making

I could sense Ari's distress but was not able to address it
Locked in my cycle of need
For someone to make me feel better

As our friendship deepened
My life-long ache gradually awakened
Arching and stretching from its season of slumber
Yawning
Still hazy and mostly numb
Yet already forceful enough to threaten my mind's reason
To myself I thought
"We're friends
    Wonderful friends
    Scorpion's Tail under control
    Dedicated to clearing her path
    To never set her on a course
    Where she might have to choose
    Between her husband and The Path"

To push my reasonable mind into blurting a lover's lament

"I need you"
When we were not lovers
Had no plans to be lovers
She insistent her marriage was sacrosanct
I worried for myself

The long moments passed in single file
Marching somewhere out of sight

She squeezed my hand
Still silent
Then "You only think you do"

How could I answer?
My ache—with no permission to exist—was deepening
Friends do not "need" each other in this way

She said she had better go
I wished her a good trip
We hugged good-bye and I kissed her cheek
Then she was gone

I was left alone
With my friendship for her
With my heart
In pieces at my feet
My work with myself for her over the past year in jeopardy

I drove home
Walked on the beach
Barely thankful for the warm winter day
Later that evening while I read pabulum
She called

She told me she did not want to leave for her trip
As we parted
She told me she was not comfortable with me needing her

She talked about our friendship
As though it were a relationship

I could just barely speak and kept saying
"I do not want to talk like this
    Over the phone
    What about Robert?"
Fearing he would overhear
Fearing he would be threatened by the tone of our friendship

I refused to pour out my heart
To tell her how I hurt
How I needed her
How I did not want to endanger her marriage
But needed her
Needed more time with her
Wanted more time with her
I refused to tell her on the phone
When he might stumble across
Our sharing
My sharing

Too late to see each other before her flight
Early the next day
We hung-up
Both miserable
I felt like she was pulling back from me
Like we were breaking-up a relationship not yet formed
I was unsure what she felt
But her suffering was clear in her voice

ANGER AND AGONY

The week passed in a wash of misery
By the weekend I was more numb than anxious

Monday came
She was due back but did not call that night

Disappointed I held off from calling her
How would she return?
Indifferent?
Apologetic?
Distant?

Tuesday more silence
I was pulled between anger and agony

Wednesday evening I called
Not able to wait longer
Sarah answered "No! Mommy is not home!"
Her tone of voice shouting
"Mommy should be here with me with our family!"

She and Sally and Robert were having dinner
I felt uncomfortable with my discomfort
With my need
Did not want Sarah to understand
"I won't interrupt your dinner" I said
Getting off the phone without even telling her
To say hello for me to the others
Or to wish her Happy Thanksgiving

The next afternoon
Thanksgiving
Ari called
Bright

Laughing
Fully there
My friend

She had missed her flight
Gotten the time mixed-up
Then was caught on Guam in the typhoon
Two days of no electricity
No water
Staying with friends of distant friends
Fun and exciting

She stopped by the next afternoon
Brought me Bali placemats
My request
And a rich golden brown silk shirt
Hand-dyed batik
I was sure I would never wear

We laid on my bed
In the afternoon
The way we had in St. Louis in my hotel room
Fully clothed and holding each other
Bodies an inch apart

She told me she had missed me terribly
Had thought of me constantly
Feeling a darkness with her the whole trip
From the way we parted

Until Guam
Until the typhoon
Until her unexpected delay
Then she was able to shake the feeling
To clear herself

She was in my arms

My friend
With unspoken love flowing between us

Whatever I had gone through was history
Forgotten the moment I saw her
Forgotten the moment I touched her

UNSPOKEN LOVE

Soon after Ari returned
Robert left for a business trip
To be away nine days

Occasional before-bed phone calls became nightly

The next Thursday evening after Thanksgiving
The girls were with friends
Robert gone
I was invited to Ari's home for dinner

Nervous
I knocked on her door
Holding seven white roses

She was enchanted
The dinner
Prepared with love
The food not quite simple enough
For my picky system
A feast of beauty and taste for anyone else
I gave nothing but praise
To her
To dinner

She showed me the house
Rented as they rebuilt their home

We watched the sunset from the lanai
Until I got too cold

We laid on cushions
Listening to Mozart again
And Vivaldi

Until I shivered
Flu still lingering
Finally asking for a blanket

Ari knew of my health problems
Knew I had been cold in St. Louis
Did not know
How easily I became chilled
How serious to my health being less than toasty could be
Especially with illness already peeking out from the covers

The delightful evening ended with a warm hug good-bye
She walked to the end of the drive
Watching as I drove off
Both smiling smiles of love under the moonlight

Unspoken love

AFRAID OF LOVE

The next night after Laureen's class
She came to my house to cuddle with me
Talking of feelings when she dared

So full of hunger for real love
So full of longing for real affection
So closed to sharing her feelings
Her real self
With anyone including herself

I felt my heart opening wider and
Letting it be
Standing a vigilant watch over my Scorpion's Tail

She told me of her Asian childhood
Summers in the mountains
Play for her
In the forest alone
Even when around people
Classical music and literature
Loves of hers

Her passion for opera
Known to me
A mystery to me
Opera was my grandmother's living room floor
Her warbling to the Saturday afternoon radio broadcast
While I winced
Killing toy soldiers

No radio or television in Ari's childhood
No rock 'n roll
No fun it seemed to me
No nurturing of spontaneity

In a culture dedicated to continuing tradition
At the expense of the individual
At the expense of freedom

She left late
The last hour spent rubbing her back
Talking in the low tones of lovers

I walked beside her car
As she drove slowly out to the street
From parking behind my apartment

She stopped just before the sidewalk and looked up at me
The still bright moon glistening in her eyes

"Goodnight" she said

I almost said "Goodnight"
Instead I leaned into her car
Closed my eyes
Kissed her on the lips
Her dry lips pressed together
"I love you" I said
Pulling back out of the car
Before she slapped me
Shocked at what I had done
Rejoicing at what I had done

She looked straight ahead
At the traffic flowing by on the Ala Wai and said
"I have been so afraid to hear that"
Then she looked into my eyes again
The unpinning of her carefully guarded heart
Reflected in her eyes
Reaching out to me
Closing off to me

The struggle between her family and heart
So visible in her rich brown eyes

LOVERS WHO ONLY KISS

Invited out again to her house
Arriving in time to hug the girls goodnight
After tickling laughing and smiling admonitions from Ari
We talked late into the night
The topic of love carried in her warmth
Her gentle heart soothing my fears without words

As our conversation died out and the music ended
We lay alongside one another
The night softened by the hour as though the last log
On an imaginary fireplace was breaking into embers
I kissed her
Lips together
Then again
Then not again
Leaving soon after without comment or discussion
Wondering again just what I had risked

Less than a week later at my apartment
Sharing our hearts after a Dream Workshop

She seeking solutions to her spiritual confusion
Me offering nothing of my own but neutrality
Trying to get out of the way
So Spirit could give her whatever It chose

Our talk died out as before
Stretched across my bed after massaging her shoulders
We reached for each other
Touching and holding back in one breath

I leaned toward her watching her eyes blur as I neared
Wondering what she was thinking
My lips met hers

Could feel her holding back her touch with tenderness
Then felt her response slowly grow

We pulled back at the same time
To look softly into the other's eyes
Feeling our hearts' loud cry

Then we kissed again
A brush of lips which grew into a full kiss
Melting into each other's arms
Our lips leading a deeper opening of our hearts
Energy flowing even and smoothly
As lover's arms held us both

Lovers who only kiss

"He never kisses me" she told me later
Burying her head into my chest

I was shocked
She felt it
"He just doesn't like to kiss" she said

A long pause later
Our pulses in harmony
She looked into my eyes
So close I had to pull back to focus

"You can have my kisses" she whispered

SILLY LESSONS

Robert returned
Our late-night phone calls ended
Christmas came
Friends of hers visited

I saw less of Ari through the holidays
Still in contact when she could

One sparkling Saturday evening
Spent with Sarah and Sally
Mexican food
A movie
Carnival Carnival
Racing from game to game
"No one ever brings us here"
"Yeah!"

Home to wait-up for Ari and Robert
Returning from their opera group
Feeling awkward
Wondering what Robert thought of my presence
Their homecoming almost awoke me
Did he think I was the new babysitter?

Outside with Robert not in sight
Ari said goodnight tenderly

During lonely days and evenings
I shopped for presents for the girls
For Ari
For other friends
For family
Grateful my mother had suggested
We just send cards this year

I carefully assembled a gift box full of
Hairbands
Play money
Little purses
Socks
Little pens
A few gemstones
For the girls in their favorite colors
For Ari
Earrings and the Far Side calendar

Writing little cards on each present
To Sarah
"Princess with a golden heart"
To Sally
"Bubbling fountain of love and mischief"
To Ari on the calendar
"Silly lessons"
On the earrings
"Love always"

The girls read their cards out loud
In front of Ari and Robert and holiday visitors
Ari later told me I was a hit

At my home Christmas night
Ari opened the Silly Lessons present
Laughed
Kissed the shiny purple card twice
Leaving imprints of her lips
Then kissed me until we almost forgot about other presents

She gave me a suitcase in a huge box
Which had sat in my small apartment
For three days until she came over that night
She liked the earrings

I felt relieved
Jewelry was always a mystery to me

More kisses
Talk of not making love
Of my warning that sex outside of marriage
Weakens the bonds between husband and wife

She told me of her conversation with Robert
In October before the trip to the World Wide
When she asked him if he had ever had an affair
His response
Was to turn red and hang his head
While sitting on the bed
And say without looking at her
"I need to keep this area of my life private
    I will explain it to you someday"

I was appalled yet said nothing
Not wanting to be the one to say
"Can't you see what that means!"
If I were just a friend with no other feelings for her
I would have

I asked her what she thought
"Either he has or he hasn't
    I don't know"

Amazed
I struggled to keep quiet
Then melted away as she kissed me
Her soft touch reaching my heart

"I'm so glad
    We're kissing
    I've missed this for so long" she whispered in my ear

Moving her lips from mine up my cheek
Without losing contact
Returning moments later

WRINKLE FREE

She came in the morning
I stayed home from work

She came after
Dropping Robert at the airport for a trip to the Kauai salon

A bright winter Tuesday
A slight coolness in the island air
Cold to me

The rest of the world busy at 10:00 in the morning
She pulled into the driveway
Smiling her smile of beauty

Light with joy
She was happy to be away from everything
Happy to be with me

Laughing at nothing and
With no other place to relax in my small apartment
We rolled on the bed
Tickling each other
My spots easy to find
Hers a challenge

"I'd better not wrinkle this
    Do you have something I could put on?" she asked
Tugging at her pressed white blouse

I searched through my closet
Finding the brown silk shirt she'd brought me from Bali
Perfect for her

She went into the bathroom

Returned in a minute
Wearing the shirt and laying her folded top and pants
On my desk

As she came back to my bed
She stretched into my arms
Her lips meeting mine
Before the rest of her body touched me or the blanket

"Your kisses melt me" she said

I rubbed her shoulders
Her knots of tension ran up into her neck

"Too much computer?"
"That and too much complaining
   He's getting so bad
   I told him last night
   If he didn't change
   I would leave him in five years"

"Five years!" I said then shut up
Such a long time seemed to make her threat meaningless
But I did not want to add my opinion to her distress

"Has it always been like this?"
"He's not as negative as his father
   But yes always"
She thought for a moment
The two furrows between her eyebrows pinched hard together
"I was very self-confident
   When I met him
   But the first two years of our marriage
   He criticized everything little thing I did
   I thought often then that
   I would leave him someday"

"And your self-confidence?"
"You already know about that
   The waver you hear in my voice you've mentioned
   That you've said sounded like a deep uncertainty
   You're right"

I stroked the back of her neck in silence
Then said "Why do you stay with him?"
Wondering if she was ready to open up

She looked at me
A gentle tear almost forming in the corner of her eye
"I don't know
   The children I suppose
   My commitment
   To our partnership
   For life"

I kissed her softly
Her lips trembling as we touched
Then she responded with a fire I had not felt in her before

My hand slipped under the hem of her shirt
As easily as brushing back my hair in the wind
Feeling her smooth skin stretched tight over her ribs
She shivered
I shivered
Then I ran my hand around to her back
As she leaned on top of me

Stroking her spine
I let my hand drift down over her cotton panties
Following the swell of her hips
Our kiss continued soft and wet
Learning more about each other

I rolled her over onto her back

Sunlight danced across her
Gleaming from her cheek
Highlighting her hard nipples under the silk shirt

"I love you"
"I love you too"
The first time she had responded in kind in the moment

I struggled with my desire for her
With my commitment to clear her path
Not clutter it

We talked about her marriage
She told me she had never been happy
With her husband as a lover
"He just satisfies himself" she said

My amazement flared
How could she be with him?
I wished in a primal way to have met her
Before she married this insensitive man

Then all thought subsided in the nearness of her
I touched her face
Smoothed the silk shirt over her breasts
Feeling her nipples
Feeling her arch into my hand
Soon the shirt was on the desk, too

She lay on her back
I lay on my side next to her
Marveling at the luster of her breasts
Of her belly
Of the roundness
Tucked away between her legs
Pushing up under white cotton

She began to take off my shirt
I helped her
She held me to her
My chest feeling her breasts beneath
The warm smoothness of her against me

I kissed her
From her nose to the swell below her belly
Stroking the insides of her thighs
"Take them off" she said
I moved down between her legs
She lifted her hips and her white cotton slid away

So softly I touched her
Felt her respond
Licked her
Barely touching skin
Then she motioned me up
"Take off your pants
    And lie next to me"

"Are you sure?" I asked
"Just lie next to me and pull the blanket over us"

I did
My hardness pressed into her hip
We lay together
Nothing separating our bodies

As we kissed our hearts joined our lips
I moved on top of her feeling her heat beneath me
My commitment to anything other than being with her
Fully
In this moment
Gone

Just before I entered her

Tenderly
So slowly
She said "no regrets"

OF OUR OWN MAKING

Two nights later
Reverberations of Tuesday morning still unsettling me
She called after her class
Laughing

Inviting her over in a breath
I walked to my car in back to move it to the street
So she could have the discretion
Of parking away from the many eyes of the many people
She and Robert knew driving along the Ala Wai
In steady streams of gossip-searching posses

As I walked down the narrow black-top drive
I thought of Ari's words
When I walked her this way Tuesday morning
After our intimacy
After being one
"This may never happen again" she had said

I nodded "Of course"
Not knowing how I felt
Knowing I loved her beyond what we shared
But may not share again

I knew we had stepped-up our karmic pace
Did not know what new chunk of effect
May now lay in our paths
A mountainside loosened from its perch
Waiting to be overcome
Or to overcome us

A challenge of our—my—own making

Then she was there in my arms

Her warm kisses saying she truly held "No regrets"

When our passion mounted
When we were a step away
From knowing more of each other again
She said "I can't while Robert's in town"

I shifted my energy
Taking a long moment to adjust
To ride the momentum
Down
To a soft tenderness
To the love we shared as
Lovers who had made love but once
Lovers who would not make love often

NEEDING ONLY TO BE KISSED

First and third Friday nights together
Became oases in the lengthening days apart
When Ari was available and
Able to get out of the house

The first and third Friday night classes we shared
Now preceded by first and third Thursday nights
Ari able to get out of the house
For her Satsang class with Shana
Visiting me afterward

We arrived at the same minute from
Different directions
Different homes
Different experiences
For Laureen's Friday class about prophecy
Learning—perhaps—to read the inner records of Soul
If and when it was in the best interest
Of the reader
Of the whole
The ability when developed to be revered as a spiritual gift
Used only with inner guidance not as a circus act
Misuse quickly resulting in problems for the misuser

This class was laying a broad foundation
For spiritual growth
For class members to develop an awareness of a gift
Mastered only by the patient
Mastered only by the pure of heart

Sometimes tedious
Sometimes esoteric
Laureen's class were always full of joy and inner unfolding

This Friday I sat fidgeting
Watching Ari across the room not watching me
Not sitting beside me to avoid rumors

After class we walked to our cars
"Would you like to go eat" I asked
She said nothing until we stood next to her car
Then looked into my eyes and said more than words can say
"Or come over" I added

"Come over" she said

We left my car in the parking lot under the big tree
Drove slowly in near silence holding hands

What felt like a short moment later
She said with regret "I'd better go"
After shedding hesitation about any conditions
Outside my apartment
Outside in each other arms

After loving slowly
Oblivious to the clock
Consumed by the waves of love building between us

Then it was late
She hurried
Brushing her hair
Touching lipstick to cover the warmest lips
I have ever known
Lips which needed nothing but to be kissed

UNFATHOMABLE

Sunday she was shaky and slightly distant
I tried to draw her out
Then eased off
Feeling her strung so tightly

I too was unsteady
The rush into intimacy
My failed commitment
Risking her steps along The Path
All caved in on me
Keeping me so busy I did not notice
My old sensitivity about fumbling vulnerability issues
Arise from the past

She left in a hurry after Service for a family outing

Monday I called
Robert answered saying "Here she is"
I asked if we could meet soon
To talk
She sounded better and suggested tea

We sat in her car talking
Never going into the restaurant

Her feelings still a jumble
Her love for me unquestioned
Asking me "Why does it have to be this way?"

I had no answers
Only my own emotional turmoil to unravel
To try to sit with
Staying with pain not a strength of mine

Our conversation ran hard
Softened for caressing moments
Then dashing off again into the limits of our experiences
So different

As an hour passed we found our harmony again
Harmony with each other
Harmony with our newly created situation

But it did not feel new
It felt like an extension of many times together in the past

Both of us had gotten glimpses of our previous relationships
In dreams
In spiritual exercises
I killed her once
My girlfriend chased her off once
She spurned me when I was a man
She left me pregnant when I was a woman
Partners in adventures ending badly

Neither of us glimpsing a time when our love worked out
Always grasping through the distortion of desperation
Settling for pain
Unable to reach out for love

"Maybe we will get it right this time" I said
She nodded "Yes"
Then clouded over as she struggled with what that might mean
The core of her old consciousness lying at her feet
Looking up with eyes as sad as Old Vicky's
The Cocker Spaniel
My granddaddy had to put in the basement each night
Because she vomited every morning

Ari's old consciousness bound her to pleasing others
At her own expense

Binding her so tightly
To the biological father of her children
She now gasped for breath

I held her
Feeling her struggle so
Feeling what she was going through
But not knowing

She did not have words yet
I did not know her well enough to understand
What was unfathomable to me

We parted on a clear note
The moon shining white on palm trees
Where we had walked along the beach
Having given up on thoughts of the restaurant
Our talk too intimate for public places

We parted with so much love I felt dizzy driving home
Her touch remained fresh on my cheek
My lips still feeling hers brushing mine so gently

TO BLEAT OR NOT TO BLEAT

"Our relationship has lost it pureness" she said "It seems
tarnished"

We stepped around a large woman carry armfuls of balloons "We
both are at risk now" she continued, struggling to find her words
"Before we became intimate we weren't vulnerable
    To each other
    Or to others around us"

We walked quickly through the exhibition hall
The annual Family Expo at Blaisdell teeming around us
A barely subdued carnival
Acutely contrasting our intimate conversation

"I would not change anything for a moment
    But the sense of loss disturbs me"
"What have you lost?" I asked

"I'm not sure
    The way we are now is wonderful
    But there is a perfectness that is missing"

I smiled
We hurried through the people and
Dodged the traffic in the parking garage
On our way to do some errands
To bring back lunch for Robert
As he stayed behind manning their booth

Amazed and shaken whenever I met him
This time was no different
Amazed he did not pick-up the tone of Ari and my relationship
Amazed he was so charming
Amazed I could look him in the eye and act naturally

Shaken I could look him the eye
Shaken by his other energy
The scalpel-sharp critical side of him
Which ambushed without warning
Shaken at what might happen when he found out

For now I was a family friend
With a growing desire to be family
Ari's friend
The girl's silly buddy
Fielding Ari's questions
Watching her struggle to understand her experiences

We got into her car
Drove three blocks then pulled over to the curb to kiss
To say hello as lovers

"Spirit gives a taste of Its sweetness
    Then often withdraws
    To see if Soul will notice Its absence
    Soul then has to choose
    Between standing still
    Bleating at what is lost
    Or work to find the bliss Itself "

She looked at me as we sat on King Street
Saturday afternoon traffic passing by
Brushing my cheek she said "Sometimes when you talk
    I want to tell you to shut-up
    To tell you that you talk too much
    But after I leave you
    Your words echo through my head again and again
    I learn from them
    And I feel your presence even more intimately"

We kissed again
Longer

Deeper
Then separated slowly
She asked me to drive
As I got back into the car from the driver's side
She squeezed my hand
Not letting go until we reached our first stop

AVOIDING DISHARMONY

"Would anyone like some tea?"
I said this wondering what the hell I was doing

The long Saturday was over
The Expo not a success for Robert and Ari's booth
The wrong show for his line of beauty products
For her imported jewelry

I was very tired and chilled in the February night air
As we stood around our three cars

Ari and I had been together away from the show
On and off throughout the day and evening

I wanted to be with her alone again before she went home
I hoped Robert would say he was too tired
Tell us to have some tea without him
That he would go on home
A wild hope
A desperate reach for her

"Sure" he said "Why don't we all go to TGI Fridays for a drink"

Not what I had in mind
But I was caught in my trap

At the restaurant I sat across from Robert
He motioned Ari to sit next to me
I wondered if this was his way of being polite

We talked business
A little spirituality
Some nonsense
Being with Robert felt like work

Sitting next to Ari felt wonderful though tenuous

He described a business venture
In which he had invested six-figures
No contract
No patents
His partner the inventor eccentric and uneven
Able to walk any time he chose I pointed out

The project was stuck
Cash about to run out
I ask him about their marketing approach
About their business plan
They had neither

The situation seemed ripe for a major lose
I wondered if Robert
Avoided bringing up the subject of paperwork to his partner
With such determination to avoid conflict
More comfortable instead
Writing checks in a blind hope the project would work out
Than face disharmony

I outlined some business principals
I had learned the hard way
He said I made sense
I offered to share past business plans with him
We said an unsettled goodnight

I reverberated with an old familiarity not quite placed and
Not enjoyed

Watching Ari and Robert
Drive away in separate cars to the same home
Pulled me in different directions

I did not want to break up a marriage which could grow

But could I?
Can anyone be responsible for another's choices?

I knew I craved Ari heart to heart as Soul

Being with her and her husband was a jarring experience
She has an edge around him I do not feel when with her alone
Her warmth receded
Fun was missing

I drove home sad and disquieted

LOVING BEAUTY

I heard her car and opened my door
As she stopped in the drive six feet from where I stood
Smiling her smile of Beauty

"Shall I park in back" she asked
"Of course"
I followed behind her watching her drive to my parking stall
I had vacated for her

She closed her car door
Slung her purse over her shoulder and walked up to me
Standing inches from my face
Eyes looking far into mine
I could barely resist the pull between us

I wanted to run across treetops to her
Pick her up in my arms
Carrying her off in the winds

Instead we hovered close
Smiles growing on our lips
We leaned toward each other gently
Lips touching
Caressing
Searching

We stood kissing
No other part of our bodies touching
Yet as much one as when making love

A moment later we burst into laughter
Grabbed each other
Wrestled standing up until we almost fell over
Then hurried back to my apartment

It was Thursday night
Her class had ended early
She had called to see if I wanted company
A formality of hers since she was expected
Hoped for

I made tea
She changed into the brown silk shirt
We curled up together on my bed
Sipping
Touching

She began to talk about her frustration
With the slow sales of her jewelry at the Expo
How she had not been able to make any headway
In marketing them
How Debbie was not working out as her partner

Ari snuggled against me, rubbing her head against my chest
My heart opening to her still more deeply

I wanted to help her find the sense of self
She had buried beneath years of criticism
To help her ignite her fire

"Maybe you need a rep" I said
"Maybe" she said "Find me one"
"Okay maybe I'll be your partner"
"I would love that" she said drawing closer

As she kissed me scenes flared in my imagination
Flashes of she and I married
The kids ours
She and I traveling the world buying for her business
As I wrote my next book

Her hands brought me back to the moment
Fantasies shimmered away
The moment more riveting than any fantasy I could have dreamt

We said good-night after midnight
Walking back to her car
The ground giving with our steps
Soft as clouds

"Tomorrow night?" I asked
"Yes" her lips shining with fresh lipstick
"I'll park on the street when I get home
You don't need to call
I'll be here waiting for you"
Ari planned to pick me on her way to our Friday class

I bent into her car
Kissed her gently
Then watched as she drove slowly out of the driveway
Part of me went with her
Part of her stayed with me

She waved as she turned onto the Ala Wai
Her taillights disappearing quickly

I closed the door to my apartment
Happy
Sad
Full of her
Lonely for her
I sat on the bed where we had just made love
Tears falling on the tile floor
Feeling so many conflicting feelings
So vulnerable
So in love with Beauty

SOBBING IN SILENCE

"I called some reps today" I said
She brightened for a moment
Then sagged again leaning against my chest
More down than I had ever seen her

Our Friday class with Laureen had been fascinating
But too long
For two people squirming to be together
Two people with a too-early curfew

Ari was lying on my bed still dressed
Not able to stay long
Sliding into depression

"What did they say?"
"Some were encouraging
    A couple not so
    I'll make more calls Monday
    Then maybe you should talk to them"
"Why don't you just set up appointments"
"Do you want me to go with you?"
"Please"

We lay together in silence for several eternities
Finally I said "I've never seen you so down
    What are you thinking about Beauty?"
"I don't know that I'm thinking" she said "I'm just numb"
"Was Robert upset this morning?"
"He was cold and distant
    It feels awful when the family is not in harmony"

"When is it in harmony?" I asked
 She thought then said "When I do what he wants me to"
"How often is that?"

108

"Lately not very often"
" You and I have different definitions of harmony"
I could feel her breathing as I talked
"To me harmony is when each person
  Is giving
  Doing what is in their best interest
  And willing to compromise
  So the whole can be more than the sum
  Of their individual energies and directions
  But when one person bends to another's will
  What kind of harmony can grow?"

She remained silent

"What kind of harmony has grown
  In your home these past eleven years?" I asked
She did not respond
"Am I talking too much again?"
Silence

I rolled her onto her back and looked into her eyes
Tears hung at the corners
"It's okay to cry Beauty" I said and kissed her lightly
Then held her

A long time later I felt her sobs begin
She cried in soft sounds heaving gently
Shaking once for several seconds

She rolled away from me
Reached for a Kleenex
Blew her nose and
Buried her head in her hands face down on the bed

I stroked her hair wishing desperately I could take her pain away
Then canceled the thought
Giving it to Spirit before I made life harder for her

After her tears dried she said
"He was so awful last night
    I almost told him about us"
"Why didn't you?"
"I don't know
    Him touching me is getting unbearable"

A picture of Robert making love to Ari
His wife
Shot through me
I let it go
Holding on to the image would only burn me

"I feel so lost" she said
"I wish I could just
    Crawl into a hole and die"
I stroked her hair
Rubbed her back
Sensing how she felt
Knowing how Spirit works
How It reveals Its glory then pulls away
Leaving Soul to flounder
Until we discover Divine Love is within each of us

I kept my thoughts in silence
Letting Ari have her experience
More than a little amazed at my control

NYLONS & SCISSORS

"Robert has to go out of town next week"
"Great" I said
She smiled
"For how long?" I added
"A week maybe ten days"

I said nothing more not wanting to push a button
I knew she wanted to see me as much as I did her
But she had the girls to think of
Had to run the house and business by herself

She snuggled closer to me and played with my hair
The blanket wrinkling under her as she shifted
We laid under crystal blue noontime skies in a park deep in Manoa
Sunday noon after Service
Having left as quickly as grace allowed

No matter how high or low she was
Ari was grace
Moving with a sureness reserved for ballerinas

I reached for the carrot juice and knocked it over
Happy to discover the plastic lid was on
She wrapped a nylon covered leg around me and
Reached up for a kiss
Getting to my lips before the juice
I did not mind

"There is only one imperfection in our world at present
    Can you guess?" I whispered into her ear
"Our situation?"
"Our situation at the moment is heaven"
"Silly me" she said "You'll have to tell"
"Your pantyhose" I shouted to the sky

"Hush someone will hear you"
"Who?
    The old guy jogging around the park?
    Think he cares?"

She laughed "Why do you dislike them so?"
"Because they imprison and distort
    Imagine a pudgy-faced burglar with a stocking mask
    That's what your Shelly looks like
    Most ignoble"
Ari shrieked with laughter
"And most inaccessible"
I said running my hands up her skirt

Her laughter turned to murmurs as we kissed again
I felt her keys on the blanket and said
"In fact I'm tempted to liberate her!"
Holding up the small Swiss army knife on her key chain
"You wouldn't dare" she taunted me

I opened the scissors from the knife
Pulled up a pucker of nylon from her thigh and
Held the scissor blades over it

We looked at the scene on her thigh as the drama mounted
Then back at each other
Then after another moment of savoring
I closed the little scissor blades in a swift movement
The steel made a crisp sound as it cut through her stocking
A large circle opened on her leg

She looked down at the hole
Shook her head
Then howled with laughter
I joined her feeling relief that she saw the humor
Surprised I had done it

I cut several more holes in her stocking legs
As we rolled around tickling and laughing
Finally collapsing in each other's arms

"I better go" she said after a while of laying together
Loving our closeness
"Yeah I know
    Too bad"
"Sure is"
She began to pick up the blanket and food
"Your legs look great"
I said admiring the pattern of holes in her nylons
"Wonderful texture
    See how much your legs want freedom
    Too bad I didn't get to liberate Shelly"

Laughing she sat down with the little scissors and
Cut off her nylon stocking legs near her crotch
When she stood her skirt covered the tattered remains nicely
"You should be locked up" she said kissing me

We walked back to the car arms around waists
Laughing and talking
Feeling so close
So much in harmony

ALMOST MOVING IN

Ari and I met with a manufacture's rep the following Tuesday
Liked the people and agreed to bring them samples
She told Robert that night
I had found her a good professional rep and
I was going to replace Debbie in the import business
Becoming her new partner

Told him?
Asked him?
I was not there so I do not know
From seeing them together I imagine she mixed her approach

Robert's response was favorable
Perhaps too occupied with preparing for his trip
Perhaps unconcerned
Perhaps feeling powerless to railroad our friendship

Whatever he felt he left the next morning
Ari was in my arms after dropping him at the airport
Both of us ignoring work to be together

With Robert out of town
We talked every night after the kids went to bed until late
Sometimes Sally would be nearby during the day when I called
And she would want to talk to me
We had great silly conversations about
Nose-picking and belly buttons
What she did that day
The sound of cockroaches crunching in gecko's mouths
Often grossing-out Ari listening nearby

Sarah and I did not have a rapport on the telephone
So when she answered
I got one syllable answers to my questions

I came by for dinner or after dinner
Snuggling with Ari after the kids went to bed
After Gudrun went out with her neighbor boyfriend
Keeping our ears tuned
For the sounds of approaching footsteps or car doors

I was taking Robert's place in the household and I loved it

When he returned after a week I suffered the loss
With a mixture of grace and heartache
I was still at the house often
Helping Ari organize and inventory her earring stock

Being around Robert was tough
He liked to complain about things and people
Making my skin crawl
Looking him in the eye was hard knowing what I knew

I was forced to be as friendly and natural as I could
Not wanting to endanger the balance
Which permitted Ari and I to be intimate
I gave away my personal space
Being as unobtrusive and neutral as possible

Watching he and Ari interact was painful
Hard enough to see her as a couple with him
Harder still to feel her sharp energy
Toward him and sometimes the kids
Horrible to see how he treated her and the kids
No affection
No support
Kidding at his family's expense
Complaining
Whining
No real communication

Often I left before I had to
Just to get away

Being with Ari away from him was golden
Flowing together so naturally

A week after he returned he left again for two weeks
I was around the house so much I practically moved in
Always wanting to be with Ari as lovers
The kids began to protest in small ways

"How come Zak is around when Daddy's gone?"
"He's around when your father's here too Sar"
"Yes but"
"We are working together sweetie
    Don't worry about it"

But Sarah did worry about it
All four of us worried about it
One Sunday after spending the afternoon and evening together
Tired
Wanting to sleep
But sleep with Ari not alone
Knowing that would be impossible
Unwilling to leave until we could be together alone
My patience slipped

At the dinner table I kept looking at Ari
Giving token attention to the girls
But finding Sal always staring at me
Watching me watch her mother

After dinner I dropped several hints
About the girls going to bed
When Sal came to me in her pajamas to say goodnight
I was reading the paper
Hiding from reality and my frustrations

116

"I always like this comic" She said pointing to "Blondie"
"Would you read it to me?"
"Another time Sal
    You need to go to bed now "

The unpracticed father in me
Losing a wonderful opportunity to give to a tender heart
To show I really cared about her
Which I did deeply

She kissed me goodnight dutifully
And padded off to bed
I returned a shouted good-night from Sar and waited for Ari

When she came to me she was reserved
Knowing she was tired I rubbed her shoulders
Asking little questions about herself
Her viewpoint on the day's happenings
About her feelings

As always I asked more questions than I got answers
Then she shared with me what the girls had said
Before going to sleep
"If you leave us for him I'll hate you"
"I'm telling Daddy how much Zak's here when he's gone"
"If he takes you away from us I'll hate him forever"
"He doesn't like us
    Just you"
    I was shocked

Ari said she reassured and scolded them for such thoughts
I felt as awful as she did
I remembered my pre-occupation with her at dinner
My unwillingness to reach out to Sally earlier
I drove home that night feeling lost
I had thought the kids were my ally

Having fun with me
Better than being crabbed-at by their father

How wrong I was

APOLOGY

The next time I saw them
I waited until they both were in their room to talk to them
I wanted to open my heart completely
To tell them how much I loved them both
How much I loved their Mommy
But not wanting to freak them out
I struggled to tell them what I felt without lying to them

I told them Ari and I were best friends
That I get tired and impatient sometimes
I apologized to Sally for not reading the comics to her
I told them I was their friend
Anytime anywhere no strings attached
And told them they did not have to be my friend
That was optional

They hugged me and said it was all right
They were embarrassed
Such warm tender hearts
I finished the talk feeling a little awkward but relieved
Until I reminded myself how hard it is
For children to confront adults
With their uncomfortable feelings
So often unclear

I reminded myself that these girls
Could have little or no training
In expressing their negative feelings
Growing up in a household
Where their parents repressed so many feelings

I began waiting for Ari to call me
Began being around their house less often
Sometimes I came by after the kids went to bed

119

Or were at their cousins for the evening
Not wanting them to be alarmed

Ari and I planned for her next Bali trip in April
Wondered if Robert would let me go with her
Decided I needed to go as her partner
Decided she would ask him when he got back
Dreamed about how wonderful it would be
To be together for a week

VISION IN WHITE

Amid so much uncertainty
A vision returned
Seen once before
Three months before meeting Ari

A new white apartment full of light
Up
But not in a high rise

I began tasting
Seeing
Feeling it again so tangibly
I often found myself surprised it was not here yet

Yet cash flow did not tell me to look for a new home

This first happened eighteen months ago
Lasting for a few weeks
Then one Saturday I packed-up
Threw-out
Re-arranged and cleaned my apartment
Which then became lighter, whiter and new to me

In the midst of this March with Ari
Trying to not neglect work
But spending business hours together
Experimenting with wholesaling to retail outlets
Tangled in the emotional fabric of her family
Sometimes strangling in my web of karma
I wondered what my vision could mean
Each time it popped up

SEPARATE ROOMS OF COURSE

The first night Robert was back Sally said to him at dinner
"How come you let Zak spend so much time with Mommy
   She's your wife!"

I was amazed to hear he shrugged off his daughter's comment

Two days later Ari met me for a lunch and told me
Robert had agreed to our Bali trip
Agreed grudgingly
"Only if no one else knows about it
   Especially the kids" he had said

I danced around the table in the restaurant
Embarrassing Ari
Kissing her flushed cheek

We began planning for our time there
Where we would go
They had lots of mileage
So we agreed she would propose to Robert
They would get my ticket I would pay for her hotel room
We would have separate rooms of course

We talked about canceling the second room when we got there
We planned to double our marketing to stores before the trip
To get a feel for the market

Ari talked about opening a store herself
I thought it would be great for her
Then realized how tied down it could make her
And me perhaps if she became mine full time

If If If
The thought was never far from my mind

My heart always wanting her

IT MUST STOP

The next several days were full of my work
The trip confirmed almost overnight
Trying to leave my borrowers' loan packages in good shape
While I was away on the trip
We were to leave in early April and return ten days later
With an eighteen hour layover in Guam on the way back
"I'm sorry I could not give you longer
Easter weekend is messing things up
Blocking out more than a week for mileage tickets"
Robert had said to Ari

Neither Ari nor I cared about the long layover
We cared only about having ten days together
Grateful it could happen at all
Gratitude comes easy when a gift is given

I stayed away from their house
Seeing Ari often during the day
As we repped her products outside the area our rep serviced

The weekend before we left
Ari and I were scheduled for a skit rehearsal at the Center
After Sunday Service
Surprised then concerned when she did not show up as planned
I left the Center the moment Service was finished
Calling her from a pay phone a block away

She answered saying she was holding on the other line
Having called the Center
Holding while someone looked for me

She sounded awful
I asked her if she was OK
Said I was worried that she had been in accident and

125

Was she coming for the rehearsal?
Blurting out my anxiety without giving her time to answer

She was silent then began crying
She said Robert knew about us
He had found out through his dream the night before
It confirmed what he suspected but did not want to see

She asked if she could come over
"To the Center? " I cried suddenly unable to face anyone
"No
   To your apartment"
"I'll go right home"

We hung-up and I stopped by the Center
Was told by three people she had called for me
I asked Michelle to please find someone else
We could not be at the rehearsal
Muttering apologies I left quickly
Raced home
Found the street full of cars and parked illegally
So Ari could park in my space
Waited and paced in and out of my door
Waited with heart beating madly

"What can happen now?
Will she leave him?
Will she tell me it is over between us?"
I wondered to myself but neither thought felt true

She drove up soon
Stopping in the driveway by my door
Looking at me with eyes wild with grief
I reached through the car window and stroked her cheeked
Kissed her gently
Then followed her car back to the parking space
I had left for her

When she got out of the car and I hugged her
She nearly fell
Trembling with fear and pain

In my apartment we laid together on my bed
Until she could talk

"He knows
    Has known for a long time
    Is so disappointed in me
    So hurt
    He feels for you
    Can understand how you feel
    But says it must stop"

I was moved by her description of his compassion
Surprised not expecting it

"What's going to happen" I asked
"I don't know"

We lay together and talked
Our emotions running up and down
She cried then laughed
I held her
Then curled up in a ball and cried for her to not leave me

She said she would never stop loving me
She still hoped to go to Bali with me
"How?" I asked incredulous
Tears falling
"We'll see"

She left
Her heart so heavy with pain
My heart dissolving

My two-year-old awakening to a bed of sharp needles

I cried all afternoon
Walked on the beach later tears blurring my vision

I called old friends in the evening reaching out for support
Something I did daily in my twenties
When I was young and emotionally reckless

Late that night unable to sleep
I wrote Robert a letter
Telling him of a love I felt for him
Which I only partially understood
Describing my pain after my father's suicide
Telling him that was the only time
I remember hurting as much as I did now

Explaining to him that
I was committed to clearing the path for Ari when we met
Determined to not get in her way
To keep our relationship a friendship only

How we edged toward intimacy over many months
After seeing how hollow their marriage was
But their marriage was not the deciding factor
Ari and I became lovers because
Our love grew beyond being able to hold back

I told him I would not stand in the way of his marriage
I would work to be only friends once again with Ari

I felt strong and clear writing to him
In touch with myself as Soul
Seeing all of us from a higher viewpoint
My two-year-old soothed by the inner love pouring through me

The letter grew into many pages

As I shared with him my spiritual experiences and
The principles I lived by
How growth and love were most important
Requiring a lot of work
How my love for Ari was unconditional

I encouraged him to push himself to grow with Ari
Since she was being stretched by Spirit

I shared my experience in counseling
Suggested he and Ari try it saying
"Everyone can benefit from some help"

I told him of learning to be more loving to myself
As I have opened to Spirit
A never ending process

I told him of my father
Of his refusing to work with his feelings
Of how gracious and charming he could be
Of how much he needed his kids
Of how much he hurt us all
Because he would not work on himself

I told Robert I was surprised by
How much he reminded me of my father
How I hoped he would act more wisely than did my Dad

I told him I did not feel guilty
I felt love and pain
Which I tried to grow through with more love

I ended the letter by sending him a hug
"From one Soul to another"

ASSHOLE

The next two days were a living nightmare
Ari called me often
I told her about the letter wondering if I should mail it
"Wait" she said
Then we decided she should read it first
Neither of us wanting to make the situation worse

I went up and down
She went up and down
Robert lost his compassion
For me
For Ari
For my love
And went down
Swamped in his pain old and new
One proclamation after another
Jerking himself and Ari around

She held fast to the claim we would become just friends again
That she wanted the time with me in Bali
To experience "true happiness"
Then she would try to work out their marriage
Saying that was the least he owed her
For twelve years of constant criticizing

He said he would change

She stopped by for a few minutes Monday morning
In tears
I held her until she settled down
Before she left she read my letter to Robert
Said it was a wonderful letter
But things were too unsure to know when to mail it

I was gallant and supportive to her one moment
While she was in my arms
Then pulling and childish a few hours later on the phone
Robert heard about my more noble side from Ari
As she lobbied to convince him we could be friends only
He struggled to convince himself of my spiritual virtues

My worst call with Ari happened Tuesday afternoon
Two days before we were supposed to leave
Two days after Robert found out about us
Not knowing if the trip was on
Not knowing what would happen next

Ari called me at work and I got angry
When I heard about Robert's flip remark
That they should use her as collateral for a loan
And if they couldn't pay I would get her
I called him "Asshole" and went downhill from there
My two-year-old crumbling into pain and fear
Pulling at her to choose me
To choose love and growth
To not go back to sleep

Late that evening Ari called
She told me Robert wanted to talk to me
He had taped our conversation that afternoon Would I come up to
their house?
She sounded like death

I could not say "No" to her
She told me to bring the letter
I wondered what kind of man would bug his own phone

The fifteen-minute drive to their house
Felt as long and as bleak
As my three hour drive thirteen years earlier
From my apartment to my father's home

132

After my sister's call on the Sunday before Thanksgiving
Telling me Daddy was holding our step-mother at gun-point I was
the only one who had a key to his house
Would I go over please?

Thirty-six hours later my father was dead
I hoped no one would die tonight
Not expecting it but aware I was taking a risk
Going to the home of my lover's husband
The local papers often recounting tales of passions flamed
And resulting assaults

I FORGOT MY HAT

Robert opened the door before I knocked
Ari was not in sight
The children were in bed I knew from her call

He explained he had to make a call to Europe
I asked if I should wait in the living room
He said "No" sharply
Then led me downstairs to their office

He apologized but explained it was important business and
Pointed to a chair in the middle of the room
A few feet away from his desk

I sat in the chair for a moment
Felt uncomfortable and exposed
Then pushed it aside and sat cross-legged on the carpet
Still holding the letter
Wondering if I was to talk to him alone

Ari came down the stairs and asked if I wanted tea
She looked as awful as she had sounded on the phone
I was cold
Said "Yes" and thanked her

She disappeared back up the stairs
While Robert talked in Swedish on the phone
I felt like a bug waiting to be squashed
My guts tight and hurting

Ari reappeared silently with three cups of ginseng tea
Sat on the chair I rejected
Ask if I wanted to sit on it
Then we waited for Robert to finish

Not knowing what had been decided between them
If anything
Left me wretched

Finally he hung up the phone and
Moved his chair into the open area where Ari and I sat
Ari said I had the letter
I gave it to him
Then we sat noiselessly watching him read it

The waiting was awful
I had to bail my emotional overload constantly
Robert clucked as he went through the pages of my letter
Clicking his tongue as he made check marks in the margin

Finally he finished
Took off his glasses and said
"Well Zak I don't know"
His voice grated
Whined
I had a hard time feeling any compassion for him

"You should have written it to both of us"
"What?" I said
"You should have written your letter to both Ari and I"
I could not believe my ears
Then remembered Ari's comments about him
Picking on little things while ignoring the real issues

He complained about me addressing my letter only to him
For several more minutes
I was amazed
If this was my competition for Ari all I had to do was wait

She finally told him enough was enough
He harrumphed and
Started going through his notes on the margins

135

My mind usually shuts down when I am angry
I could see the same thing happening to him
It was the first time I had watched it happen in another
I knew then without a doubt
He was sitting on a huge pile of old pain
Buffeting him around whenever the garbage got stirred up

"I really thought you were a spiritual person Zak If I had read this
letter
    yesterday Well...
    But after hearing you on the phone today
    I've got your call on tape you know
    Would you like to hear?
    It shows the real you Zak
    You're just a phony after all"

I sat still on the floor looking up at him
My arms folded around my knees bent up in front of me
I wanted to look up at him
I wanted to stay vulnerable for Ari's sake
Knowing it would be too easy for me to clash with Robert
Sitting on a chair trying to get the upper hand

I let his words fly by
Seeing I would not get far tonight
His mind was made up
What was I there for?
To absorb punishment I decided

My mind drifted back to the last conversation
I had with my father
The evening of the day I drove to his home
When he was holding my step-mother at gun-point

When I arrived no one was home
I went inside the house
Found Dad's old hunting rifle

His only weapon
And got out of there fast taking the gun

I waited until he and Jay-Jay returned
Then drove by several times
Agonizing over just when I should go in
Terrorized about confronting my father
Something I had only tried three times in my life
Each time a miserable failure
Neither of us able to express our upsets constructively

Both of us unbearably miserable when not close to the other
He miserable with his old baggage
And his unwillingness to face himself
I miserable being close to him
Because he was in so much pain
And because I could not protect myself from his hurt
Loving my father was like hugging a fan
I got cut-up a lot
Being apart from him was worse

When I walked through the front door of his house
He looked up surprised and said
"Hi Zachary
    Nice to see you
    Didn't expect you for a few more days"

Jay-Jay was watching TV
Said a quick "Hi" as she darted back toward their bedroom
Not acting like someone awaiting rescue

"We're just getting ready to watch Billy Graham
    If you'd like to join us" my father said to me
    Not something I would do on a good day
I said "No thanks Dad
    I need to talk to you about something"
His eyes narrowed

I went on before he could object
"I hear you've been holding Jay-Jay at gun-point"
My heart tore at my chest
Adrenaline pumped through me until I could barely think
"Zachary I am going to have to ask you to let this alone
    It's our business"
"I can't do that Dad"
He got angry as only he could
"All right then come outside and I'll tell you"
His lips were tight
He waved his cigarette like a baton punctuating his words

I followed him outside
He stopped in the middle of the walk
His back to the two large fur trees guarding our yard
Which I had struggled to trim all through high school
Right on the very spot where the FBI had arrested me
Eight years and not many days earlier
For refusing induction into the Army

He told me about his Miracle
About how he was waiting for Jay-Jay to repent her adultery
Planning then to shoot her and himself
So they could go to heaven together
He said he had been shown that he did not need to kill her
Just be willing to make the sacrifice
Like Abraham's test with his son Isaac
"So everything is all right now" he said

I knew then I could do nothing more
Jay-Jay had not asked for protection
I had the gun in my car
The man who when he was twenty-one
Had told his proselytizing Christian mother
"Jesus is just like Santa Claus"
Was now watching Billy Graham and working Miracles

138

"I forgot my hat" I said
Running into the house then back out again
I passed by him too angry to look at his face or say good-bye
Before I got to my car I heard him say
"You act like you wish I had done it"
I yelled "No!"
The last thing I said to my father
The last time I saw him alive
In the physical body I knew so well and loved so dearly

As I drove away I realized how tired I was
How worn down I had been for years by his threats and pulling
Beginning before high school when I had heard periodically
"You're all I have son
    If anything happens to you I'll kill myself"

I did not wish him or Jay-Jay dead
But I was tired of his threats
"Shit or get off the pot Dad" I thought

Twenty-four hours later he did

Perhaps thinking of my father helped me
Put Robert in perspective
I came back to the present
To find he was trying to bargain with me for Ari

I could not have been more disgusted or revolted
What did she see in this man?
I looked at her
She seemed so far away
So miserable

I reminded myself this would not be anyone's finer moment
I worked consciously to keep Robert
And his accusatory off-the-issue rambling in perspective
Without feeling the panic of past confrontations

But I could not say much
No matter how many words I used

He was insisting I reconcile the person on the tape
Who pulled at Ari
Telling her Robert was awful for her
With the person who wrote the letter
Mixing spiritual principals with promises of non-intervention

I could not
It wasn't until two days later that
I saw my higher and lower self struggling
Saw my human consciousness pulling at Ari
And criticizing Robert
I as Soul could see the bigger picture

It is the struggle each of us goes through constantly
In varying degrees of awareness

I wish I had been able to tell Robert then
"Look I have good moments and bad moments
   I am both those people and more"

I could not promise Robert
Ari and I would never be lovers again
That I would truly not stand in the way of their marriage
"I will try my best" I said

My words only exasperated him
"You people on The Path are all alike
   You're rubber bands!" he yelled

Later Ari and I had a good laugh when she told me
Before I had arrived and in response to his demands that
She assure him we would be just friends
She had said "I will try my best"

I told him that I saw him
As a man like myself with an old cache of pain
Unresolved
Which he expressed indirectly
By criticizing the world around him

I told him I thought he had a lot of work to do
And if he really wanted Ari back fully
"You will have to work your ass off"
"Yeah yeah I will change" he said

I left soon after
He actually smiled and held out his hand
Appearing to me so unable to sit with discomfort
That he sought reconciliation with me
His wife's lover

"Good luck" to both of you I said and left

Ari later told me how much that hurt her
Did she think I was saying I leave you two here as a couple?
I never asked her what she thought that night
Too much happened too fast
I know she did not ask me to rescue her

THE DEAL

The relief driving home that night was deafening
My emotions swarmed
I felt angry
At being subjected to Robert's small self point of view
Sad for Ari
Sad for him
I know what it is like to carry crap inside
I felt a little hope for the long view
"If Ari keeps growing she will out-grow him
    Because I don't think he will face himself" I thought

I felt hopeless in the moment
How could we go to Bali now?
I could not even think of what lay ahead if we did

Sleep was elusive
I awoke in a sweat with an emotional hangover
My body ached all over
My head pounded
I was weak and shaky

I made it to work late in the morning
Ari called from a phone booth
To say she had a couple hours free
Could I get away for lunch?
"How are you?" I asked
"I'll tell you when I see you "

I walked out to meet her
Wondering if it would be for the last time

She wore dark glasses and had her head tied up in a scarf
Looking like she had been up all night cleaning
After attending a week of funerals

142

"You don't look so good" I said and kissed her cheek
"If I look as bad as you
    Then I should be left out in the sun to die" she said with a hint
of a smile
"That's a thought"
We burst into laughter draining away our tension
"Sounds pretty bad to me" she said
"Sounds terminal--let's get out of here"

She drove into Manoa Valley
Toward our favorite health food market

"What happened after I left last night" I finally said

"Nothing good
    We fought for most of the night
    He wants me to never see you again"
"And"
"That's not what I want"
"Come to any decision?
    Is this the last time I see you?
    What about Bali?"

She was silent in her way for blocks
I felt like I was sliding slowly down a long sharp edge
Waiting to feel the bite of metal Then she said "We can go to Bali"
"You're kidding!
    Why?
    How?"

"Because I insisted on it
    I told Robert I would leave him
    If he prevented us from going"
"Wow---what then?"
"He agreed
    On the condition that when we return
    We only see each other on Sundays at Service for a year"

"A YEAR!
   Do I have a say in this?"
"You don't have to come to Bali
   But I hope you will"

I shut up fast
As awful as the deal sounded
I knew it was Ari and Robert's decision
How to handle their marriage
My decision was how to be involved with Ari
With what she had leftover
Until
If

Feeling like I was going nuts inside I swallowed it

We stopped and picked up our sandwiches
Then drove to the nearby park
Once we spread out the blankets
We forgot about the food and held each other

"I don't know whether to prepare for a wake
   Or a celebration" I said
"Me neither
   But our flight is tomorrow evening   If you want to go"
"Of course I want to go!
   Are you crazy?
   No way could I pass up a chance to be with you for ten days
   No matter what coming home means"

She kissed me like we were alone forever
Kissed me and rolled me over
Unbuttoning my shirt
Running her hands all over me
Her passion overwhelming both of us

144

GO WITH LOVE

I left work soon after she dropped me off
To go home to pack and rest
I was so tired from the tension

The next morning I saw Laureen for a treatment
She hugged me like the dear friend she was
Squeezed my hand as my tears fell
Telling her what was happening with Ari
Then she said "I want you two to go to Bali and
    Not think about anything or anyone else
    Let Spirit handle Honolulu and
    Whatever it is you are to return to
    Go to Bali
    Go with only love in your hearts
    Be sure and tell Ari this word for word
    Now get on the table
    You need a treatment
    And this one's on me"

I made it to the airport
Ninety minutes ahead of our flight time
International check-in is two hours before departure

I had spoken to Ari briefly at noon
Told her Laureen's words
She said she would be there but I wondered if she would
Could Robert really let her go?
Go away with her lover for ten days?
I don't know that I could
Then I reminded myself that he and I are different people

I waited by the agricultural inspection station
Hawaii restricts live products leaving it
To keep medflies out of California

I waited and waited looking at my wrist
Which had not held a watch since high school
Wondering why the new airport was built
Without one public clock
I tried to read watches on people as they walked by
Then she was there
Rolling her suitcase along behind her
Looking like a professional traveler

"Where's Robert?" I asked
"He wouldn't come in
    I told him he should at least say hello to you
    But he refused "
"Well I 'm glad
    Let's get out of here"

We checked in easily
Got to the gate and boarded in minutes
Settled into our first-class seats
Were given water and orange juice by the flight attendant
I held Ari's hand and my breath
Waiting for the plane to lift off
Hoping nothing would pull us back at the last moment
Not sure I could stand going back to my apartment alone
If the flight was canceled

Ari seemed sad and distant
The plane finally pushed away from the gate
Rolled out to the runway and left Honolulu behind

We raised the seat arm between us and cuddled
An hour later we were laughing
And deep into five across tic-tac-toe
Played on a full page covered with lines
The noise of the airplane drowning the past
Washing away our pain and fears

147

BALI #1

The Year Of Living Dangerously kept running through my mind
As we stood in line
Stood in a rickety wooden building without walls
The nighttime humidity oppressive
Guards standing around with rifles looking oppressive

I saw Mel Gibson and Sigourney Weaver living through
Death and upheaval in Jakarta
The capital of Indonesia
One island away from where we stood in Denpasar, Bali

The movie ten or more years old
Its events fiction?
I did not think so
But I did know of the trouble in East Timor
An outer island in the Indonesian chain
A people persecuted and repressed by Sukarno or Suharto
Or whoever was the benevolent ruler of Indonesia today
Benevolence had its blind spots evidently

Ari and I passed through immigration without event
Hand in hand sweating from the heat
From the turmoil we had left behind
From the anguish we faced upon return

"I want you both to go with love
    To live completely in the moment
    This trip is a gift of love for you" Laureen had told us
Holding each of our hands in both of hers
At an unplanned lunch together the day before we left

In this area of the world where violence
Can appear out of nowhere I sensed
Especially to a midwestern kid with soft eyes

149

Unwise in the ways of third world countries
Spirit wrapped us in Its love
Whisking us through the airport and
To a shuttle to the Sheraton
The little van shuddering with each bump
Blowing stale air conditioning directly onto my head
Until we finally convinced the driver
To turn it off

The people at the Sheraton Lagoon at Nusa Dua Beach
Welcomed us graciously
Our room was far away from the large open hotel entrance
The valet wheeled our bags through the halls
To the door of number four-sixty-three

The room opened up before us
Two steps down from the entry
A king-size bed covered in white floated between
Walls and floor and ceiling of lush dark woods
To our left the bath waited on the entry-level
A shower with Jacuzzi looking out over the big bed
Cantilevered like a treehouse

Down and into the room
Bags set in the corner
A tip and a thank you
A warm hug and a warmer kiss
We opened the sliding glass door to a small lanai
Which overlooked a tropical playground of
Pools
Lagoons one of which had its own beach
Lighted paths
A waterfall
Palm trees and greenery
And the ocean
The South Pacific shimmering in the moonlight
Washing up to a gently curving sandy beach

Echoing the shape of the moon above

A lovers' paradise
A gift to two lovers

We unpacked
Too tired from the trip and the days before
To do anything in a hurry
We showered then soaked in the Jacuzzi
Soaping and massaging
Touching with delight and tender care
Always a part of Ari and my loving
The first time we were able to enjoy each other unhurried

We slid into bed together
The crisp white sheets wrapping around us
Making love slowly
As though we would be together all our lives
Losing the trauma of the past four days in Honolulu
Along with the tensions and tiredness of travel

Fully in the moment
We were determined to love as if there were no more tomorrows

BALI #2

The morning awoke us gently
Soft sunrise melting our sleep away
Giving us both what we had wanted
What we had cried for
What we had loved for

Waking in each other's arms

We stretched in unison like synchronized skiers
I kissed her shoulder then her neck then her lips
She tasted sleepy and wonderful

In a moment she was out of the bed and into the bathroom
"Getting up so soon?" I asked
She was back in my arms
Before I wondered about her not answering
The toilet rumbling somewhere in the distance
Her breath toothpaste fresh

"Do you want me to shave?"
"Later" she mumbled through our lips

We showered and dressed agreeing to rest the whole day
For both of us
For my lungs still wheezing from the airplane

Later we left the room walking hand-in-hand
Down the tiled hallway
Down three flights of the open-air stairway
Down to the ground floor and across the winding pathways
Separating lagoon from pool
Small bar from another pool
The beach from one restaurant being cleaned before lunch

We walked in the surf like newlyweds from Iowa
Then found our way to the larger restaurant
Serving a free brunch
Fresh juices in glass pitchers set in ice
Carrot
Melon
Pineapple
Guava
Watermelon
Orange
Lemon
Grapefruit
Apple
Papaya and more
Fresh fruits many new to me
A cereal and croissant bar
Two chefs in white hats making omelets pancakes and waffles to
order
Large silver heated servers full of
Scrambled eggs
Rice
Sausage
Potatoes
And an Indonesian dish with a choice of
Hot peppers shoyu or peanuts for garnish

All this food
As much as we wanted
To be eaten sitting next to a lagoon
Fed by gurgling waters pouring over rocks
Waited on by a group of young people
Whose smiles grace and courtesy
Enchanted an already enchanting morning

Ari never wanted to leave
I agreed

After brunch we walked the beach both ways
To our left down three or four hotels
To a group of local people
Offering to sell the simplest of wares
T-shirts
Plastic toys
Flowers
Sarongs
Coming out of the bushes
Smiling but hungry for money
Just beyond this group the beach became rock and uninviting
So we turned back
Retracing our steps
Passing our hotel and continuing on
Leaving the beach to walk overland across a jetty
Ending in cliffs
To the next beach which ran in a short arch
Ending in another set of cliffs
We crossed another narrow strip of land and
Found a third beach which stretched out for miles

Not far down it we found another hotel
With a labyrinth of pools
Finally shaking the ever-present local self-employed
Apparently shying away from hotel property

We swam in the pools of this unnamed hotel
Watched Japanese newlyweds play and blush
Ran quickly across the toe-burning brick surfaces
Beside the water
Rested on plastic cots
I feeling stronger by the moment
My lungs soaking up the heat and sunshine
Ari beginning to purr with pleasure
The reality of Honolulu fading

We played in the ocean

Hugging intimately until a group of young kids from Australia
Interrupted our fun with their own craziness
We laughed and floated with them
Batting beach balls back and forth
Slowly drifting away from the group in each other's arms

Feeling a little drained
We walked back across the two hidden beaches
Through the unrelenting local people
One offered to sell me a purple and green dinosaur
Some lost toy of a vacationing two-year-old

We napped
Falling asleep with our lips touching
Her breath caressing my cheek
As I slipped away from the physical world

The day was still with us when we awoke
I massaged her with oil
Teasing between her legs
Then said "after a swim" when she wanted to do me

We tried the pool downstairs under a late afternoon sun
Played like the kids in the ocean
Then discovered two small basketball goals
In one corner of the free-form pools
The balls were all clustered around a water intake
Up a small channel leading to another pool
We raced there
She won
Then raced back
I won because I held her by her swimsuit

She had never played basketball
I had played a lot as a boy
Learning to jump well for my size
Never able to overcome terrible shooting

With her lack of experience
And my shooting eye
We were about even
Except I knew how to play defense
A concept foreign to Ari

Soon I proposed a handicapping system
The moment she touched the ball it was hers and
I could do nothing to interfere with her shot
As soon as I had the ball she could do anything to me and
When she touched the ball I had to give it to her

Great rules
But they overlooked her training to never interfere

After teasing her about her non-existent defense for a while
She loosened up
Thirty minutes later she was all over me
Hanging on to my shoulders when I went up for a shot
Grabbing at the ball
Grabbing at me
Her best technique was to pull my trunks down
When I jumped to shoot

Once she got them off me entirely and
Held them over her head like a trophy

My heart melted as I watched her come alive
Cheering her on as she stepped into herself
Throwing off her lifetime of self-repression
For the sake of values learned to suit others' desires

She won our game to fifty
Which lasted well into the evening
My heart so happy to be with her
I helped her more than myself

BALI #3

The next morning Ari phoned the transit company
She had used in November
The driver she asked for was out of the office
She was assured he would pick us up as requested at noon

We laid in bed
Until we had to hurry to brunch before it ended and to be ready
for our transit

Her driver did not come with the little van
Instead a bright-faced young man introduced himself as Bagus
Showed us to the just-washed bus
Presented us in broken English to the driver Erawan
With everyone smiling and nodding we set off

Halfway to somewhere Bagus ask us where we wanted to go
Ari was trying to understand why her driver was not available
And told Bagus "Kuta" without more thought
A couple miles later realizing
She needed to stop by a bank
Instead of the money changers in Kuta

I was fiddling with the air conditioner vents
Trying to redirect them away from me
Acting nonchalant about Erawan's driving
Until his U-turn caught my attention

He drove across a grass median
Separating what might have been the only four-lane highway in Bali
And blended in with
Three scooters a Mercedes and two large trucks
As precisely as a diskette slipped into the drive on my laptop

I knew Ari was not immune

To the excitement of close-tolerance driving
From periodic exclamations she made when I cut it close
While driving in Honolulu

She and Bagus were absorbed in conversation

Our four lanes narrowed to two lanes
Without the protection of a median strip
As we headed back the way we came
The scooters ahead of us
Keeping their tires exactly on the center line
Making it difficult to pass I thought
Until the Mercedes lurched around them kicking up dust
From the shoulder on the other side of the road

A mass of oncoming traffic was growing larger as it neared us
I wondered if the Mercedes would make it
Then Erawan followed
Pulling out into the oncoming lane into certain death it seemed
The Mercedes now a first line of defense against
A large delivery van and herd of scooters
Bearing down upon us

I tapped Ari on the shoulder frantically
She turned to me
Saw my mouth and eyes wide open looking straight ahead
Looked forward and said "Oh my"
As the Mercedes folded back into our original lane
As Erawan followed
The oncoming scooters having moved over
To the far edge of their lane
To avoid us
We missing the van behind them by a foot
As it made as much room as possible for our van
Without running off the road
Which would have meant
The destruction of three ramshackle road-side stands

Selling little of anything from almost bare shelves

No one honked screamed or yelled in anger
Everyone went on their and our way
Ari said to me softly "Fun yeah?"
Bagus grinned still hanging over the back seat talking to Ari

I nodded and mumbled and squeezed Ari's shoulder
She leaned into me kissing me on the cheek
Bagus grinned broader
She whispered into my ear
"It's wonderful to be here with you"
Then held my hand and began talking to Bagus again
Her Thaiglish and his Balinglish blurred in my ears

Taking several deep breaths and
Tiring of trying to dodge the jet stream from the AC
I asked if we could shut it off

Erawan complied with a toothy smile
Turning around to look at me in the back seat
Nodding his head several times
As we continued down the highway
Without the benefit of our driver's eyes on the road

BALI #4

We began our scouting of Kuta by mid-afternoon
After finding one bank closed
Another open
After stopping for fresh juices
The day's heat and humidity quickly sucking us dry

Kuta was a blur of little shops and dusty roads
Of traffic moving slowly on impossibly cramped roads
Made worse by sidewalk and draining ditch repair
Erawan often having to pull in his rear-view mirror
To pass an oncoming vehicle

With the little van parked we walked and looked until
Still tired from our flight and other realities
We asked Erawan to return us to the hotel
He dropped Bagus by the office on the way
Twice we watched oncoming traffic approach in large bunches
Using our lane to pass slower vehicles
I began to get used to it as my confidence in Erawan grew
"The Balinese drive the way fish swim in a school" I thought to
myself

At the hotel we skipped a dinner neither of us hungry
Laid in each other's arms after a shower
Went down to the pool for a short swim
Soon returning to the room

I massaged Ari with oil and felt her slipping away from me
As she lay with her face buried in her arms
For a long time she would not respond to my gentle questions
Would not rollover

When she finally did turn on her back and looked at me
I saw her nearly lost in grief anguish spilling from her eyes

"What's wrong Beauty?"
Nothing
"What are you feeling?"
Silence
"What can I do for you?"
She shook her head
"It would mean so much to me if you could tell me
    What you are going through"

After a long silence she began to talk
Mostly saying "I just don't know what to do"
Talking of her feeling of being caught in a trap
Wanting to break free of it
Wanting to just disappear
"Feeling so awful" she said

I held her
Talked to her about the effects of a lifetime
Of holding in feelings
About what I went through when I began
To clean out my old garbage
Talked about different experiences of other people
Setting out on The Path

Talked about how Spirit cleanses us
How we begin to work off our karma
How life speeds up
Often leaving us feeling overwhelmed

The only way out surrendering to Spirit
A lesson which must be won every day
A step to be re-learned on many different levels

I held her until she held me
We made love with her tears dried on her cheek and
My tears flowing fresh across both our faces
Tears of deep joy unknown before

Tears of haunting grief
Of pain past
Of pain to come for both of us
Trying desperately to push aside the realities of Honolulu
To live in the moment with Ari
To love in the moment with Ari
To give fully to this wondrous women

BALI #5

The days flew by like hours
We shopped during the afternoons
Buying little
Looking a lot
We kissed under the stars
Skinny dipped in the big lagoon late at night
Teased and laughed

Try as we did
We still cried when one of us lost the moment
To the reality waiting in Honolulu
Of seeing each other only on Sunday mornings at the Center

The deal did not seem real to me
Love was not something to bargain over

Not knowing what was coming except pain
I was the one who turned to tears most often
Ari more experienced at repressing her feelings

One evening too close to our departure for my comfort
I lost my inner struggle with my little boy
Lost out to his white-knuckle grip
On the pain of being left behind
It happened to him long ago and he had yet to forgive

I began by asking Ari
If she was really going to honor the deal with Robert
"What are you going to do?"
Something we had talked about often
Something she had no answer for
I could not imagine not seeing her
She felt the same way
We left it at that until the evening when I pushed it

164

"You're going to go back home and go to sleep aren't you
    I risk my heart to pull you out of your shell and
    All you can say is 'Thank you but I made this deal'
    You must like pain to choose it
    How can you just walk away
    From our four hundred year love?"

Those were the nice things I said
By the time I was warmed up
Ari had buried her face in her arms soon to be in tears
Badgered by my inability to say
"I hurt more than I can stand
    I don't know how I can function not seeing you
    Won't you please reconsider
    Won't you please honor our love"

Instead I pounded her with my anger
Until she had to get away for a walk

I followed her
Both of us wretched

We waded in silence into the big lagoon
Swimming back to the waterfall holding hands underwater
As the sheets of water pounded our shoulders

We went to sleep late that night
After I apologized
After we talked a little
About why she can express only part of her feelings
We hugged and caressed
Finally letting our physical bodies rest

I awoke with an emotional hang-over
She awoke sunny-faced with only a hint of shadow in her eyes
Which she dropped by mid-day

165

Coaxing me back to self-respect with love and forgiveness

BALI #6

The last days became frantic
As we searched for the right products for Ari to buy
Trying also to find something for family and friends
I not able to buy for the girls or Gudrun
Since I was still in Honolulu to them

We reached for the idyllic mood of the first days
Before the tears came
Before the need to accomplish set in
Before return came nearer
But we fell short with each attempt

Our lovemaking became frantic and dulled
Steeling ourselves for the gauntlet of fire to come

We played tennis one sunny afternoon
Taking a break from Kuta and the stores
Before our last plunge
Which would be the major buying time

It was Ari who suggested tennis
I went along wondering
If I could even get the ball over the net

Fifteen years earlier when I had last played
I was in great shape
Yet still unable to hit the ball well enough
To enjoy the game
Preferring racquetball

But play we did
With a short lesson thrown-in by the hotel assistant pro
I was able to hit the ball occasionally
Surprising myself

Dismayed my hand was numb within the first few minutes
My grip used to be so strong from picture framing

The hot sun baked us
Until we ran for the pool and more basketball
Ari was savage on defense
Delighting me
We discovered we had been using the wrong balls
Undersized volleyballs just barely smaller than the rim

The little basketballs were very small
Fitting easily through the hoops
By now we were used to the heavier volleyballs
The change lost on our hilarious shooting
We were beyond caring as we splashed and molested each other
I breaking our rules by harassing Ari as she shot
Finally winning a game to twenty-five

The next day we stormed Kuta
Buying sack-loads of beaded clothing
Ari carefully picking each piece for design and workmanship
A lot of crap to be sorted through
Mixed in with good merchandise

One shop owner kept calling me "Boss"
I began calling Ari "Big Boss"
Then "Big Boss Honey"
To make it clear to him he could not use his sexism on her

She laughed but largely ignored us
As she focused on sorting through his whole inventory
To find the right pieces
And make clear the needed wording for the labels

After the buying was done
We hassled with shipping companies
Trying to find one who would prepare the visa

So we could hand-carry the goods back on the plane

One company could get it ready for us
But we would have to stay three extra days

Ari faxed Robert explaining the situation
Asking if he could re-schedule the flights
We were not hopeful
About his willingness or of the availability of flights
In the midst of Easter weekend

The next day upon return from Kuta
We found a message from him to me
Asking us to return as planned the next day

I was very unsettled that he would respond to me
Not Ari
It seemed such a slap to her

We finalized arrangements with another shipper
Had a strange and strained dinner
At an Italian restaurant above an antique store
In the middle of what seemed to be rice patties
Outside of Kuta

Brushing away mosquitos and our heavy hearts
We tried to enjoy the food

The last day we went into Kuta briefly
Finally found shirts in my size
Ari wanted me to have

We returned to the hotel
To the beach
To the pool
To the bed
All our movements done in gray silhouette

A silent pantomime of times just past
Acted out now as blackness descended

Packing
Checking out of the hotel
Saying good-bye to Erawan and Bagus
We made it to our flight
Passing through immigration as we did before
In the open-air wooden building
Which now reminded me of stockyards

Finally leaving Bali
Cushioned in thanks-to-mileage first-class seats
Hand in hand
Holding on to the very last moment
Not having kept our agreement to live fully in the moment
To enjoy our stay in Bali as though Honolulu did not exist
We left with the consolation
That we had made love more than we cried

EN ROUTE

After the gentle delicacy of Bali and its people
Guam was a shock
Knowing only an hour in its airport on the flight down

With Easter overloading the airlines
We had an eighteen-hour layover
In the land of 11,000 snakes per square mile
And counting

I had booked a hotel from the airport a week earlier
Where we headed with relief after the long first leg
Of our run back to reality and heartbreak

Room 303 of the Hotel Mai' Ana was our second shock in Guam
Near the airport looking very comfortable in brochure photos
Recommended by a flight attendant
It was a seedy transplant from Highway 41 in Tennessee

Too tired to look for another place to sleep
Taken aback at paying seven dollars
For a cab ride around the corner
We asked to see another room
One that did not reek of mold

Room 127 did not smell as badly
So we tipped the fellow helping valiantly with our bags
Showered
Lay in each other's arms
Slowly stroking the other's cheek
Wiping away tears seeping steadily of their own accord

We fell asleep at dawn
Not bothering to wonder what time it was in Bali
Our bodies' last point of reference

171

The hotel operator told me it was noon when I called
After awakening
Ari cuddled sleepily next to me
Rubbing against my body in a soft rhythm
Which soon turned to passion

We made love as lovers for the last time
Not knowing what was to come
Throwing the sheets to all corners of the room

We began tickling each other while making love
Creating a riotous swing between laughter and passion
Hitting a plateau of near-orgasm
Which held while time slipped away

Wanting to keep all sensations alive for as long as possible
Not willing to face the end
Until swept away in love tears of joy and grief
Both crying "I love you forever"
As we were swept away in our ecstasy
Finally laying spent in a tangle of soaked sheets
Grinning
Our lungs heaving for air
"Rats" I said and we both howled with laughter
"Too bad" she stammered
    "We'll have to do it again"
"Call Robert
    Tell him we can't leave yet
    We have to make love until we get it right"
"Too bad we picked such a lousy place
    To quarantine ourselves"
"Yes
    But what a wonderful quarantine"

Ari untangled herself from my legs and the sheets and
Stretched out along my body

172

Our sweat acting like a super-conductor for our love
Heart to heart
Soul to Soul

"I love you Turkey"
"I love you Big Boss Honey"
"I will love you forever"
"I have loved you forever"
"I don't know how I am going to live without you"
"I will always be with you"

I could not hold back the tears any longer
Grief welling up from my gut where my two-year-old resides
Nurse-maiding his forty-year-old hurt

As my body shook with sobs I felt Ari join me
Crying for ourselves
Crying for each other
Crying for our love lost again
Another lifetime in which we have failed
Having met too late
For circumstances to permit us to join our lives

TOUCHDOWN

The taxi driver pulled into the driveway cut-out
Along the Ala Wai
Opened the trunk and set my bags on the sidewalk
"Twenty-one dollars" he told me
With a look in his eye saying he too knew grief
I gave him twenty-five
Grateful for his sensitivity and his silence

I dragged my bags into my small apartment
Opened the stuffed mailbox as a neighbor walked by
Pulled out the creased letters and magazines
Closed the mailbox
Closed my door
Partway through a quick sort of the mail
Sitting on the bed sweating from too many clothes
Realizing I was still dressed for the plane

I stripped
Picked up the mail again
Then dropped it
Letting it scatter on the floor
As I doubled-up in pain
As real as hot metal being shoved into my body
When I left my last body in World War II

I dimly heard myself scream
Felt my head pound as tears triggered my sinuses

Later I became aware of moaning
Holding my stomach
Laying naked on my bed
In my little room
Where Ari and I had become lovers
Where we would never love again

Saying over and over softly
"Ari where are you?"
  Ari where are you?
  Ari where are you?
  Ari where are you?
  Ari where are you?"

Ari was not with me in the physical
I could feel her touch
I could taste her breath and her lips
I could hear her laughter
I could wrap myself in her love
On the inner

In my human consciousness I was alone and miserable
Missing my lover
My spiritual twin
More than life itself

I wondered what Spirit could possibly have reserved for me
What could I have done in past lives
To create this living hell for myself

I wondered how I was going to be able to function
To go to work
To go to the Center
To smile at strangers
To ever love another other than Ari
Who was at this moment back with her husband

I wondered how I was ever going to survive

DESTROYING ILLUSION

I went out
I was doing fine
Running hard to stay in front of the emotional dogs
Staying busy
Rowing on my rowing machine
Playing tennis with the wall
Working
Writing

Seeing her in little bits of time snatched
From the bindings of the past

I went out
I was doing fine riding the after-Seminar wave
Then I could not handle it again
Choosing to jump off the crest
Losing the high energy

Now my emotional body darts glances
One way then the next
Poised over darkness
Wondering what will fall?
What have I created?

Living on the razor's edge

I pass sensuous women everyday
Today's white spandex too tight to ignore though
Returning from missing a frustrating client
A ball of energy rolled over me
A moment's fantasy
A moment's relaxation
I went out

The women were boring
I went through the motions of feigning interest

176

They did not care as long as I fed garters with dollars

I thought I had taken a step up
I thought I had left this behind
Will I ever?

Now what?
An hour cruising through the dance bars
Will not ruin me but
I will see the results
Somewhere soon in my life
I always do

I already feel my momentum shattered
Anxious to reclaim it
Knowing an upward direction can only be built
And then be rebuilt in small steps
More practice ahead of me now sitting with my shit

We never get away with anything
Though it may seem so if we don't see it come back

When we are able to relate today's Effect
With yesterday's Cause
We can tie together Cause and Effect
Destroying illusion

STRETCHING

This morning while folded over double
Doing stretching exercises
I saw the connection
I saw how I had created the ball of energy
Which had rolled over me the night before

In early April just before Bali
I had visited a client
Whom we saved from foreclosure last year
With a short-term private investor loan

A fellow who made all the right promises
Following through on few
My job now was to steer him into long term financing
Protecting our private investor who wanted his money back
Who was entitled to getting his money back
Who did not want to foreclose

Two foreclosures are hard to explain

The uncooperative borrower had shattered another agreement
I lost my temper
Leaving without finishing our business
Saying maybe he would see me again or maybe he would not
My two year old had the reins

I knew this outburst would come back
Everything does

Long forgotten and buried in the agonizing beauty
Of traveling with Ari
Of returning home with Ari
Of crying with Ari
The Effect of that early April Cause
Came rolling back at his house last night

He was not home
Having to come back again was bad enough
His wife
Usually warm
His boys
Usually playful
Were cool almost cold

She managed a weak smile
When I told her to tell her husband
I wanted to find out how he was doing
Discuss how I could help them

That sounded better than warning of impending foreclosure
Which I had done in a recent telephone message
But did not erase my earlier actions

I left disappointed
I would have to come back the next night
Disappointed there was no resolution
But not owning my own creation
Not dissipating the lingering energy

The after-effect was the ball of energy
Which opened me to the too-tight spandex
Which I rode out to the dance clubs

Handling this Effect
As poorly as I did the early April situation
Which Caused the Effect in the first place

I TOLD HER

I told her
I knew I would
I didn't expect
It to happen before lunch today
I didn't expect to see her today

I did expect her to react with caring reproach
To support my disappointment in myself
To understand

Driving to Restaurant Row
I said "I am shaky and wounded
In one area today"
"Because of me?" she asked
"No
    Because of myself" I felt her relief

A few minutes later in the parking garage
I told her I had gone out
I explained the lingering effects of the anger
From early April
How I had handled the effects
As poorly as I handled the client when I left in a huff

She closed down
A blossom a moment ago
Now wilting under her own pain

"So where do you draw the line next time
    Do you find one of those street girls"
Her quiet piercing anger stung
I sat silently feeling my own temper seethe

I wanted to run
To scream
To say hurtful things to her

Instead I stayed with my feelings
Determined to do nothing more to wound her
To not push her farther away

"No
    I already drew the line well short of street girls
    I did not touch anyone
    I did not make any dates
    I passed through a couple clubs
    Looking
    Pushing dollars into garters
    It was pretty boring

"I'm not happy I did it
    It has thrown off my inner rhythm
    My physical body is just now
    Settling down from the pounding it took
    From the music and the vibrations
    I lost a couple hours of sleep and
    Stepped down from the high I was on"

She looked at me
In a way that passed a blow torch across my heart

I was ready for whatever
I knew I would pay for what I did
Just did not know how

I ask her what she was feeling

"If we were in a normal relationship
    Would you still feel the need to do this periodically?"

"No I would not" I sat with this quietly
Not wanting to encourage guilt for her
"But my sexuality is my responsibility
    Not yours"

I asked her again what she was feeling
She was silent for so long
I thought she was not going to answer
Then she said
"I feel badly you have lost a battle and
    I feel badly I cannot help you with this now"

"You choose not to" I said
Wanting to keep us both clear
About the choices we were making

We talked longer then she reached for the keys
To shut off the car and the air conditioning
"Let's go eat" she said

I could still feel the edge in her voice
"No let's not" I covered her hands on her key ring
"Please sit with me a little longer
So we can work this through if possible"

We did
We talked of our different values
Of how we probably held each other
In unrealistically high esteem

We talked about growth
How it is not straight up
The "battle lost" is just another step
Another experience which I would work hard not to repeat
Which I have passed up many times

When she reached for the keys a second time
I asked her to wait again

Looking into her eyes
The cassette storage console separating us
I asked her to kiss me

She looked at me
Her eyes quieted but still in pain

I asked again resisted leaning over to her
We sat silent and still
Cars passing on their way to the exit
Shining their lights through our windshield

I wondered
If she was going to be unable to get beyond this

She smiled
"Should I wait until the cars pass?"
I had no idea what she was talking about
No others cars existed for me
"What?"

"The cars" she motioned with one hand
As the last one drove passed us
She leaned over to kissed me
Full of passion
We kissed one of our
Never-want-to-end kisses

Her lips slid across my cheek
Her mouth open
A faint moan deep within
"I missed you so much yesterday and last night
Remembering I did not tell you I loved you the day before"

I remembered she had not said "I love you" back to me
As she drove off after not playing tennis

We have different "I love you" rhythms

"Why didn't you?" I asked
"I was trying to be neutral"
Her voice in my ear pushed me gently past my hurt

Feeling the strength of my commitment
Not to throw my anger at her
I realized I had not

My reward flowed into my ear
Purring in time to my heart
"I love you" she said "So very very much"

After another forever kiss I said
"I'm so sorry
I didn't realize hurting myself
Hurt you so much because it hurt me "

POUNDING SURF

Laureen was back from her thirty day trip
Through the South Pacific

So good to hear her voice on the phone
She asked how I was
How Ari and I were doing
I said "Great" and told her about
The hard time the day before
How I had truly stayed with my stuff

She told me she had been aware
Of my pain several times on her trip
Helping me on the inner when she could

I had often felt her love wrap around me
Felt the Mahanta's protection blazing in white light

The moment with her on the phone
Pierced my heart with gratitude
Opening it more to Spirit

She said she was very proud of me
That Ari and I were growing so much

It was a wonderful talk
A few hours later I called Laureen again
After falling apart inside
My emotional body suddenly self-destructing

She was out but called back later
We both laughed about how quickly
Spirit snaps the calm tide into pounding surf
When we declare how strong we are

Another vote for neutrality in all things

UNBEARABLE

Had I written this when I came home an hour ago
It would have been flooded with tears

Mr. Nicola called needing help
A gentle man of overwhelming sincerity
In foreclosure because he takes much better care
Of his adult children than himself

I spent the time with him because I could help
Spirit has put me in a place where I'm able to give service
To those willing to learn about themselves
To do all they can for themselves first

As I am now I breathe tears
The white hot poker buried in my heart

Another tennis day
She was late but came with
Her adorable spoiled two-year-old niece Shelley

A court was free
We hit the ball across the net when we cleared it

Light hearted
Playful
Happy
I asked her about seeing her tonight after her class

She had not said no
Twice this week when we talked about it
Did I have false hope?
She seemed to have decided to live our secret life
At times mocking her husband's childish demands

She shook her head
"Tomorrow night after Laureen's class we can have dinner"

186

"Only dinner" was the message

My heart sank slowly then plummeted out of reach
I did not stay with my feelings
My quick reactive moves into anger and blame
Were blunted by recent work
But I did not stay with my stuff

We stopped playing tennis
Retired to the park outside
Throwing balls to Shelley
Watching her shriek with glee

Ari told me in her half clear way
Building up to it in steps
She told me
She asked me to just be friends
To not be lovers

She said she should do this to give Robert a fair chance
She said she should do this
To keep from hindering my spiritual growth

I lost it
I refused to be only a part of what we were

I railed
I shrieked the desperate shriek of a mortally wounded man

After the intimacy we had shared in the past week
This sudden reversal and her calm coolness
Tore at my heart like acid on lace
As I sat in my small apartment
Tennis having disintegrated quickly

If I thought she did not love me I would hurt worse
But only for a while

Rejection is tangible

Watching her choose safety and comfort
Choose to bury a very special love
Choose to walk away from me
From us
Because there was finally a little peace in her home
Was unbearable

I know I am attached and very unneutral
Am I unfair too?
When I am hurting it is so hard to see clearly

If I were neutral I would be able to say
"This is a tough one
    Beauty
    But I support you
    And if this is what you need to do I'll be fine"

I'm not neutral tonight
I'm a crumbling teary-eyed lonely lover
Loving another alone in my apartment

Knowing I am blocking Spirit
Feeling so much pain
Angry but grateful to my father
His suicide sealing my fate to stick it out
No matter what

DESPERATE

She called at nine
I was still on the downhill side of my tears
Ready to say how miserable I was

Hearing her voice
Hearing that she had gone home to a huge fight with Robert
Over being late
Because he wanted to have a family dinner
Hearing that she had not made it to her Dream Class
Lifted me out of my troubles
Seeing her hardships from a higher point of view

I saw her pulled so hard between Robert and me

She had left the house
Telling Robert she needed to talk to Shana
Our friend who facilitates Ari's class

Ari called me instead
Asked me if I could meet her for half an hour
Of course I did

My two-year-old wondering if she was going to finish
The job of severing the cord

My adult self calmed my child
As I sang HHHHUUUUU driving to meet her
Reaching for Soul's high viewpoint

She was soft warm and so down
So torn apart
Feeling that she was living a lie whatever she did

I mostly shut up
Healed quickly
Apologized for losing hold of my hurt

189

An hour later we parted
I suggested we set the next two weeks aside
Not making love

She agreed
I asked her how she felt about doing that
She said she would try anything

"I'm desperate"

HER FREEDOM

I dreamed I beat up a very close friend
Helped them to their car when they regained consciousness
Then told them they fell down some stairs

A coach knew I had taken something special from this friend
Had put it in my pocket

He used his detector to find it
Forcing me to surrender

I recounted the dream into my hand-held recorder
Which I keep by my bedside though
I have never transcribed
The many dreams I have recorded

I took the dream into contemplation asking what it meant
In moments I was shown the dream was about Ari

She was the friend I had beaten up
With my feelings thrown on her to escape the hurt

I stay with my stuff much better than a month ago
Yet The Path always narrows

The coach was my spiritual guide
The Mahanta
On the other side from my anger
From my act of taking something special from Ari
Her freedom

By pushing her toward actions I hoped would soothe my
discomfort
I limited her freedom

SNOW WHITE

Great day at work
Our office is now six
Bob's and my commitment to staying very small is threatened
Happily
The company beginning to choose its own course
As each of us carefully thrown together
Learns each other's strengths and weaknesses

The white apartment confirmed
I am so amazed
Saying little as the incestuous affair unfolded

A loan to a policeman eighteen months ago in foreclosure
Letters of commendation sold me
Bob and a new private investor too

Later we all learned from another policeman
The fellow was a great cop but "a renegade with his bills"

Our private investor was forced to foreclose
Then buy the unit to protect his interest
From being eaten away by legal bills and an uncertain market
For Bishop Estate leasehold condos

The apartment had been refurbished before the loan was made
New white carpet
New white tile
New white refrigerator
White paint throughout
About the time I first sensed my new white home

Standing vacant all this time waiting for events
Waiting for me?

The investor is renting me the apartment
His purchase closed yesterday

My commission check arrived yesterday
Credit and reference check done two days earlier
My current landlord and I in agreement
On how and when I'll move

The snow white apartment
Up but in a low-rise
Not important in the big picture
But a thrill today
My first place in ten years
Which I have the health and funds
To choose and shape to my needs

TWO WEEKS

Home from work and awake from a moment's nap
My thoughts on Laureen's class only ninety minutes away
Ari would be there unless problems at home kept her away

She had said as much the night before

My heart anxious over what the evening held
Or would not hold

Sitting at my desk my heart beating with anticipation
I talked with a client on the phone
Finally reaching him after a death in the family
Needing to see if they would agree to loan terms
Proposed by a private investor

A little beep in my ear told me another call was waiting

Ari's wonderful voice said "Hi"
She sounded very happy asking if I was ready for class
"Can I pick you up in ten minutes?"
"Yes!"

I finished with my client quickly
Half showered and ran out the door to the corner
Where Ari said she would be

We arrived at the street sign at the same time
She was so light so happy
Said she had found neutral ground
Was not affected by either Robert or me

So great to see her this way
We did errands

Laureen's words
From our second conversation of the night before

Echoed through my mind
Telling me the situation may soon resolve itself
My test is to be so grateful for the love
For the experience
Humility pours out of me and around me
Flooding my life

"It will be easy" she said
    "If events go the way you want
    The really hard test will be
    If it doesn't"

I pictured waving good-bye to Robert
As he left our home after visiting the girls
An image not new to me
Easy to be open and full of love in that setting

Then I visualized myself in Robert's place
Visiting the family as it is now
Sure that no change was soon contemplated

My heart slammed shut just thinking about it
I asked inwardly for more strength before I faced that one
Or its equivalent

I shared Laureen's words about humility with Ari
Without describing the two scenarios

I told her seeing her so desperate the night before
Sobered me
That I felt stronger
From proposing the two week time-out from intimacy
That it helped relieve my feelings of helplessness

She squeezed my hands
Smiling a deeply happy smile

Class was absorbing

Laureen talked about her experiences on her trip
Showing how Spirit was always at work

In Fiji she watched the Bobbies raise the flag
She did a spiritual exercise centered around seeing
People with Golden Hearts with red roses shining
From the middle of their hearts

As she watched the forty or so island policemen
Who traveled all over the island
She felt her heart burst wide open
Then saw each of the Bobbies
Radiating a throbbing heart of gold
A vivid red rose held so lovingly within each heart

She knew that these men would take this love
Throughout the Island
She felt touched by Spirit
Blessed to me a part of such opening

She said it was the highlight of her trip

After class Ari suggested we drive up to Tantalus
To be alone and watch the city below

We passed the good lookout points
Because they were full
Occupied with one car on an evening when one was the limit

We found a wonderful spot
Under the pines farther up the mountain

Crawling into the back seat to hold each other
We soon were surrounded by a misty rain
Falling apologetically

Ari told me
Curled together in the back seat

She felt she had shattered trust between us
By asking me to be just friends

She told me she had become aware
She had not been living in the moment
But was doing so now being together whenever we could

She said "On the drive up here
   I felt like being with you
   Was all I needed
   Which I have never felt with Robert
   Yet I have so much baggage
   And responsibility with the children"

She told me of his response to her question
Asking him if he had ever "Loved someone so much..."
Leaving the sentence unfinished
Knowing he knew she was talking about her feeling for me

He said "Oh that never lasts"

I know the part which never lasts
Know it too well
I also know the deep intensity which does last and builds
When two people share
Love
Laughter
Friendship and
A spiritual affinity
Learning to give service together

She also told me
She was very happy when I refused to be just friends

"Two weeks have never
   gone by so quickly" she said later
In the back seat on Tantalus astride my lap
Husky voiced

Moving in a rhythm identical to mine

CAN IT BE TRUE?

Can it?
Three days rolling smoothly by
Ari's leap into the moment leading the way
Setting the tone for my step away from anguish

A subtle bliss underlying each moment

Saturday she called
On a day when I was not expecting to see her
Doing errands while Sarah takes her violin lesson
Ari's main errand was to call me
She was light and happy on the phone

The next day at Sunday Service she told me
She and Robert had shared better than in years
Than ever

My gut tightened
Then I remembered to thank Spirit
For her
For the experience
I relaxed as she continued
Telling me her new harmony with Robert
Made her love for me even greater

I know how this works

Happy
Relieved I had not followed the pain into garbage
We stepped up into a new level of love
Buoyed by accepting a small amount of true detachment
Letting Spirit flow greater

We had lunch in the park
She had arranged her free time with Robert

Amazed I played and shared
Listened and loved her

Parting nearly on time
She meeting Robert and girls
For an afternoon hike

I went futon shopping
Then home for a nap and packing
Riding on a magic carpet of subtle bliss
Sailing on the currents of Spirit
Powered by gratitude
Love
And the willingness to experience life
The willingness to grow

Some days it all clicks
Life in the moment
Easy then to see the bigger picture of constant change
Pain only a result of resistance to change
Pain only a result of holding on to fear

SIDESTEPPING WHINING

Monday she called at work
To say if I had been home she would have dropped by

I was having a quiet productive holiday and was able
Remarkably
To sidestep regret and whining

She said she might not make tennis
So many things to do for her trip tomorrow to the Big Island
To put some Bali items in the salons

We talked about my new apartment
About futons and pillow covers
About her day trip with her husband

I moved through the silly fear of her traveling with him
Away from me

I was late in arriving at the practice court
Not expecting her
Ala Moana Park crowded on Memorial Day
Palm trees
Open grassy areas
Mostly filled with
Volleyball
Cook-outs
People laughing

She was there
At the practice wall
Sweating
Having gotten there early
So much for expectations

There was even a free court
We hit two shot volleys for a while

"I have an excuse" I said
Hitting the last ball into the next court
She looked over the net then said "I'm waiting"
"I didn't warm up"
She laughed
Hit her ball into the net and said
"I think I warmed up too much"

Soon we were out in the park lying on the grass
She read me a poem by Faust
Beautiful
But—to me—the words echoed with an old consciousness
She loved it
We both getting better at accepting the other without protest

She showed me fabric from Bali I had not seen before
Possibly for pillows
"The first trip" she explained at my confusion

She told me of her dream
The night before
Holding small birds in her hands
One of them purple
Afraid to let them go in her house
Too many holes
Some large enough for a cat to come inside
Looking for somewhere to put the birds
No cage big enough
She put them in a white envelope
When finally a large enough cage was available
All the birds in the envelope were limp

The birds were her family
The purple one was me

I asked her what the dream meant to her
She said she felt she was holding onto everyone

So tightly
We all were suffering

I offered another viewpoint
Careful to label it as mine
Her meaning the more important since
We each are the best interpreter of our own dreams

I shared with her that
While she had been telling me about the dream
I had seen the little birds
As the freedoms she was winning but still unable to trust
Unable to reach for flight in a seemingly hostile environment

"But maybe you aren't ready to surrender fully
It's a process of many small steps for me"

She smiled her far-away smile
Then squeezed my hand and
Burst back into the moment
Quizzing me about my plans for the apartment

"It sounds wonderful "she said "for your girlfriend"
"I hope you'll visit often"
"For your next girlfriend"
Her eyes sparkled

Her words felt like little fish hooks
Ripping through my solar plexus
"Is that what you want?
   For me to find a new girlfriend?"

She had played this way before

Silent
Looking into my eyes
She said "If I can approve her"
Quickly followed by

"No I don't mean that"

"If you don't want me
    To find a new girlfriend
    Will you please stop saying so
    When you say that I feel pushed out of your life
    While you are pulling me
    Towards you at the same time
    I thought we had worked this through Friday evening
    You living in the moment
    Us being together whenever we can"

She hugged me
"I won't say it again
    Sorry
    Staying in the moment gets tricky sometimes"

I agreed
We talked more about it
Kissed and bounced back to lightness

I walked her to her car
Making plans for Wednesday
Perhaps she could make some time in the afternoon
After our lunch with Laureen
To visit the Futon Store
To look at their pillow fabric
To see if some of it would work with hers

She began to get into the car then stopped and
Looked across the roof at me
Her beaded baseball cap so cute

"Sorry I said dumb things"

I shrugged my shoulders
Arms out-stretched
Smiling

"You have plenty of room to do so
  After all the dumb things
  I've tossed your way"

She smiled
Radiated
Love flowing from our hearts to each other
In waves nearly visible

CHAOS INTO ORDER

Ten pounds of pennies
A year of credit card receipts
I began packing without cleaning the house
Without straightening the house
I just began

It was time
The move had its own momentum

A day and a half later
Seven boxes later
My desk was cleared
The table by the door
My staging area for every next day
For the past four and half years
Clutter free

This little furnished studio in Waikiki had been my home
Longer than all but two other roofs-over-my-head

Nine built-in shelves over my computer
Full of five years of cartoons
Seminar flyers
Books
Cassettes collected
Notes about things to do
Things to write
Things to not forget
Last year's tax forms in a pile undone
Ten pounds of pennies
A year of credit card receipts
All this and more

Gone
Into boxes
Into drawers

Into the trash
Chaos transformed into order

A NIGHT WITH NO DAY

The day of her Big Island trip with her husband
My silly fear shaken upside down and left outside
To dissipate on its owns terms
I was busy signing my lease
Meeting the carpet cleaners
Staying in touch with the office

So tired after three weeks
Of falling asleep slowly and waking early

The Seminar come and gone
Writing again
Work
The move
Ari
Running on 300 volts
Playing tennis
Rowing on my rowing machine
Two protein drinks a day
Rocket fuel
Hoping I wouldn't crash

I fought loneliness but
Drifted down with the evening
Silly fear returning undissipated
Did the laundry
Aching to share daily routines with Ari
Life in the moment slipping away

I pushed through wishing she would call
I did what needed to be done
Then wished she would call

Past midnight the sense she was home again in her bed
Calmed me
Not thinking about whom she is sleeping with

Part of the bargain
Part of the commitment to her growth

My goal to give her the time
To grow as she will
Knowing if she and I were to be together
We both must unfold into a new consciousness

As long as we both work toward our own unfolding
Ari wins
I win
Spirit wins
Whether we are ever together in the physical
Or not

This thought from a higher viewpoint
Of dim comfort on this night with no day

SCOTCHGUARD WORKS

So early in the day
Yesterday
Hours before she left for her day trip to the Big Island
Ari sat alone in her home while everyone else was asleep
Writing to me while I was sliding into despondency

"Zak
 It is past midnight
 All is quiet but my heartbeat with thoughts of you
 Remembering your words earlier today
 You said you were very tired
 I dare not to dial
 To disturb your sweet dreams
 You are with me anyway
 More than just talking to me
 How I miss your embrace
 My whole being is filled with your love
 Just several hours ago you kissed me
 But it seems years have passed
 Till Wednesday...
 It will be years more until then
 Must I wait with beating heart and
 Constant thoughts of you?
 Till then
 Goodnight"

I learned of her feelings
After my Wednesday morning of uncertainty

Unsure if she would pick me up for lunch
Unsure because Monday she told me
She might lease a small commercial space
For her Bali items
For a line of silk shirts
Hand-painted by her

She decided she wanted this space last week
Only to be told someone else had just put in an offer
Very disappointed
She had struggled to detach for a day
Then was able to put it into the hands of Spirit

"Now the store may come back" she had told me Monday
The prospective new owner was short on capital
His plans for the space not in line with management's
Leaving her eager for the next meeting
Which might be at any time

My anxiety evaporated as she drove up

I learned of her letter
After our lunch with Laureen
Full of laughter and
Serious talk of working through karmic attachments
To be able to leave the physical for good this lifetime

While we ate Laureen shared with Ari
Her experiences with her first marriage
Which taught her so much

Ari opened up
About her feelings of conflict
Between old and new consciousness
Of her recent success with staying in the moment
And her experience of the balance being fleeting

"Yes
    You have to re-win it constantly" Laureen said
Then suddenly saw the three of us at dinner in the future
Happy
In Asia
Korea she thought
A clear vision
A prophecy different than what Spirit usually gives her

Then she brushed it aside
"Maybe we'll be doing it on the inner"

We talked about the strong karma
Between Ari and me
How we knew we had been together many lifetimes
Not able to get it right
"Maybe this time" we each said to Laureen
As we have often said to each other

In Ari's car in the parking garage
Waiting for Laureen parked above us
To drive by so we could go to the top level
To look at color swatches of fabric in daylight
To hold each other in one of the many places
We have found to be together
Alone

"Maybe she already has left" Ari said
I agreed
We backed out and drove up against the flow
Of cars filing out of the garage after lunch
On the next level we passed Laureen
Going down and out
Cars so close we were as near as at the table

"I don't believe you two!" she laughed
"Going to get it right this time?"
We laughed
"You're red" Ari told me as we drove on

I hardly ever blush

We decided to forego the rooftop and drove
To my apartment

After making love on the white carpet
A square of Bali fabric beneath us

To keep the light flow of her period from the carpet
Holding each other engulfed in our intimacy
She told me she had written me a letter
"It's in my purse"
I slid from her to get it
Discovering bright red on both of us

I went to the bathroom for tissue
Nothing in the apartment but us
A JCPenny catalog and fabric samples and squares

I washed myself off but did not dry
Careless as a small boy
Unaware I was dripping small spots of red

Through the bedroom to her

She cleaned herself
Then gave me the letter
So touched by her feelings
I threatened to spank her for not calling me
Whenever she wanted to and could
She had more consideration for me
Than I do for myself

We made love again in the middle of the living room
Finding afterward that the fabric square was not thick enough
To keep red off the never lived-on
Just-cleaned white carpet

Scurrying to clean it up she discovered both
My little trail from the bathroom and
That Scotchguard works
As I watched her I felt helpless and guilty like a small boy
Yet so pleased she cared

We went to the Futon Store and
She found different fabrics for the pillow-covers

Confusing me totally for twenty minutes
Then it was clear
I liked her choices
Fresher than what I picked-out
Fabric ordered
We went to look for new shoes for her
Her old shoes all becoming tight

Later in the evening
After a tender late afternoon good-bye
I found I was again in the moment
The ache of yesterday
The anxiety of the morning
Gone

So easy for me to be neutral
When I get what I want

I plunged back into packing
Enjoying the present

BEFUDDLED

My two-year-old awoke first this morning
Hanging on to my side
Gnawing
Just where he had been the night before

I stepped lightly through the morning
Dodging landmines and snake pits
Ari called as I was shaving

"I'm surrendering
    The way a man in a leaking boat bails water" I said
She laughed and asked what the problem was
"Emotional
    What do you think?
    I miss you" I said
A happy bubble still in her voice
She told me her meeting with the mall management
Had gone well
Someone there knew her husband

My little boy wanted nurturing
Not stories of successes with hubby

I let my child take control then watched coward-like
As he whipped both himself and me
Then Ari
Dragging her through the mud of my discontent

Dipping into anxiety and jealousy
I accused her of relishing her comfort
She parried my first jabs with cool disdain

My two-year-old seethed with rejection
After asking in his own obnoxious way for love

Did I make it clear to her in the beginning

That I was hurting and needed some attention?

Partially I think
I did not ask for help outright
Did not beg for sweet words
I wanted her to read between my lines
I wanting upfront reassurance that all is well
From the woman who instinctually
Withholds her words of kindness and longing
Until well after we first meet
Whether in person or on the phone

Often I pull at her to open up and
She tells me to handle my own feelings

When she opens I care for myself better
When I nurture myself she opens up

Tormentors or teachers for each other
Our choice

We talked for an hour after I wounded her
I felt how low she became and reached out
Nurturing her for a long stretch of her disconsolance

Then she was better
Though no bubbles in her voice
I explained to her about validating feelings
Again
I agreed I had lost it and apologized for hurting her

"Just because I have a need
    Does not mean you can fill it
    But when you can soothe my two-year-old for a minute
    When you can be upfront with your feelings
    Not relying on you calling me to be the only evidence
    Of your love for me
    Then we can pass our rough spots with more harmony"

We hung-up with "I love you"

In a moment I was out my door
Late to meet the telephone installer at the new apartment
Forgetting to shave

I remembered asking Ari
Days?
Weeks?
Years ago?
Not to rely on telling me she loved me
Or she was always with me
But to show love through her actions

Now I had told her the opposite

Was I being hypocritical?
Was my two-year-old
Twisting each situation to meet his in the moment needs?
My adult condoning with smooth justification?

Befuddled
I blundered into the day
Living the garbage of my anger

HEAD IN ASS

Work was shit
Like the after-taste from vomiting
My morning swing into anger hanging on

A client who was a frustration to everyone in our office
Was about to close a loan with a lender we brokered for her
But her loan amount did not cover our fee

She had previously agreed to a payment arrangement
Including a dump truck as collateral
Now she was waffling
Wanting an advisor to review our promissory note
Wanting to see the copy of her brokerage agreement
Having done nothing she promised

We talked of possible litigation

The note wasn't finished
We were waiting for her to fax a copy of the truck title
Before printing out the final draft

I looked in her file to check the signed fee agreement
She had faxed back to me in late January
It was not there

Where then?

I went through the file again page by page
I went through our original fax files
For January and February
My gut sinking
Feeling angry and irresponsible

Soon it was time for my appointment with Laureen
She hugged me when I walked into the office
"I hope you know the points

To help me
Get my head out of my ass" I said

On the white table in the white office
She checked my pulses and said
"You can stop this you know"
"I know"
"You can focus on what takes you down
Or on what lifts you"
"Yes"

"And you love it"
I was silent
"You didn't want to hear that did you"
I tried to say something clever but nothing came out
Hearing the tiredness in my voice I said
"I must be getting something out of this
    I know I'm creating it"
"You sure are" Laureen said
Laughing her wonderful rich laugh of complete abandon

We talked and laughed
She warned me against running myself down further

The move
Writing
Ari
Work
Inner work
Unable to sleep more than a few hours
I was running on 300 volts
Holding up very well for what I was doing
But still putting up too much resistance to handle it

Slowly the treatment and her love
Helped me lift out of my funk

My beeper went off

Ari
I called her
She was home alone with time to talk
"Where are you?" she asked
I told her and asked her to page me at 3:15
I would be home or on my way by then

I was happy to hear from her but felt a little on edge
She had sounded low again
Wondering what her tone could mean
I held onto my anxiety for the rest of the treatment
Fearful of more pain with Ari
More stuff I could not stay with

Laureen did not mention my shift
I was grateful
I know she felt it

I left Laureen's office repeating her last words to me
"You are a complete and total being
    Happy, full of light and love"

MAYBE THE FLU

The answering machine
Clicked off as I walked through the door
No message

Five minutes later she called
Not paging me

She told me she was sitting on her lanai
I pictured the ocean
Its varying shades of blue and blue-green
In the background behind the sharp slope
Running down the ridge from her home
Then back up the other side a rifle shot away
Green with tangled growth

She had gone back to bed that morning after our talk
Slept until eleven and done nothing so far during the day
She felt fragile over the phone
"I feel so close to you and weak from our argument"
She laughed "Maybe I just have the flu"

"Maybe it's both" I said

As we talked I stayed clear and detached from fear
I soothed my two-year-old and
Nurtured her mostly by listening
Ari talked of her swings that morning
During our conversation and afterward

I admitted the problems my outburst created
Humbled by my grief during the morning
Seeing my anger manifest

She said she felt better and was about to say something
When her tone changed
"He's coming

I'd better go
I love you"
I lingered in loving silence after she hung-up
Amazed at how much I learned being close to her

I called work then stayed home for the afternoon to pack

Later I called Michelle
To tell her I found the all-cotton rugs she wanted
In JC Penny's catalog

We talked longer than I expected
I lay down for a nap
So tired
A moment before sleep came the phone rang
Ari
"Want to play tennis?"
"What's happening?"
"I just want to hit some balls
    Work out my frustration"
"I'll be there in fifteen minutes"

Throwing off my tiredness
I met her at Kaimuki Park
She was hitting against a narrow practice wall
Next to courts which had no nets
"Nice nets"
"Just our kind of court" she laughed hugging me

We played against the wall hitting in turns like racketball
I won the home run derby nine to two

Then we sat on the steps which led up to a playing field
Cuddling
Talking quietly
She had her energy back
Was only a little pensive
Talked more about the store

"If I get it
    I will have to make a fast trip to Bali"
"Why?"
"To stock it
    I don't have much left"

The retail space she hoped for was tiny
Her wholesaling since two her buying trips
Through the winter not outstanding
Her comment did not make sense

My kid had an
About-to-be-berserk-with-expected-pain moment
Feel to him
I ruffled his hair
Said to him silently
"It's ok
    We are a complete and total being
    Happy, full of light and love"
Amazingly he mellowed

Ari said the management company called
Wanting to see their financial statement
"Hopeful sign" she said
"It's a good thing Robert was with you then
    My financial statement would not help much"
She laughed
I laughed
Our hearts open
Love and trust flowing
Between us

ASK AND BE SHOWN

After tennis
After leaving Ari
A strong warm energy
Flowed throughout me

Home quickly to shower
At the office by eight
For my appointment
Message on the office machine
Postponing meeting

Sweeping away annoyance
At not being called at home
At not being saved the trouble
I left

Free of obligations
On a hot Friday night
My hormonal control
Lasted two blocks

The warm energy of moments ago
Now raging
Pulling me to a dance club
"No, I don't want to do this!"
But I did
My will losing the contest

Just before I gave in
I gave it to Spirit
Wrapping myself in white light
"Take me where you want me, Spirit"
I said out loud
"Give me the experience You want me to have"

Immediately I saw a dance club in my inner vision

Turned left at the next light
And drove there
Feeling that I had lost another round

Parking behind the bar
I walked into the back door
Of the Nite Lite
No one asked what I wanted to drink
So I saved
Four dollars for a glass of water

Then I saw paramedics on stage
Men
Fully clothed
Bending over a figure
Curled nearly into a fetal position
Covered with a gauzy sheet

I heard someone say she had fallen
"She's done this before" someone else said
"No, I think she's broken her hip"

The girl lay on the stage
Screaming as the paramedics rolled her over
The music still loud
Two other girls still dancing
Dollar bills feathering their garter belts
In a surreal mourning ritual
For a fallen sister

Then she was on the stretcher
Carried out the door
Within arm's length of where I stood

Spirit told me I could go home
I did
Asking what it all meant

Opening the door to my apartment
Only packing waiting for me
I wondered if
Spirit had used me
As a silent vehicle
Putting me where I was needed
When I asked

I did not wonder
That Spirit was also showing me
How crippling
Dance bars could be for me

Even I can see the obvious
Sometimes

A CALL OF CLOSENESS

A call of closeness
Forty minutes
Lasting a moment

Ari phoned as I was packing
She was alone again
At home

We spent the time
As though waking up
On this Saturday morning
After sleeping late
In each other's arms

Then she was gone
Sweetness lingering
My heart light with her breath
In my ear

As I began to pack again
I wondered if we had been bugged
Not wanting to upset
Her fragile peace at home
Not wanting to risk
Another war
Which might lead to seeing her less
Or none at all

SUNDAY MOVE

Furniture moved yesterday
Scott's strong shoulders
Making it possible
In one trip
Today Ari was to help

Looking forward to the
Time with her with
Muted anticipation

Not too far to fall
If plans changed

Sally came with her
To the 9:00 HU Song
Reserved
Unusual for her bouncy self
Self-conscious
Sarah with friends

Between the HU
And Sunday Service
We drove Sal
To her cousins'
Her choice to spend the day there
Instead of with us

She flushed when I told her
How beautiful a woman she was going to be
Now she was stuck with being
A cute kid
"A cute big kid" she corrected

As we pulled up to the drive
She told her Mother
"I don't think you should

Hang around with this guy
He's too crazy"

A funny comment
From the girl who
Called me "Fun-man"

We laughed
Brushed it off
Hugged her good-bye
She mugged for us
As she called upstairs
To be let through
The security doors

Then we drove away
Talking about Sal's concerns
Briefly

A day with Ari
A feeling of being one
With something greater than myself

My mind knows I am a whole being
Happy, full of light and love
Able to experience
Divine Love
Shut-off from this
Purest Love
Only by my own resistance
By my own attachments

Twice I have experienced
Love
Higher than anything before
Love between myself and Spirit
Love for God

Normally I am aware of the
Tailings
Of Divine Love
When I happen to pass through
A moment of neutrality

Loving Ari
Opens me
Shows me there is Love
As I feel the outflow of Spirit to her
As I feel Spirit flowing back from her
And accepting It
Letting the Breath of God
Nurture me

This was our Sunday of moving together
We made love on my old bed
Before beginning
Laying together
Until the afternoon could have disappeared
During a pause in our lovemaking
Ari said, looking into my eyes
"I can see how much you love me
 Can see how much I could mean to you"
"How much you do mean?" I asked
"No, how much I could mean"

Then we worked hard and fast
So she could leave on time

Cars unloaded
At my new apartment
We talked
Almost made love again
Living the glow of
Loving each other
Until she was late

WEAVING

A possible lunch
Did not happen
Ari was late
Her mother's doctor's appointment
Taking far too long

We sat together
In the parking lot next to my office
After loading her bar stools
Back into her car
Leftover from the Seminar
Retrieved from the Center
The day before
Only to be left at my old apartment
While we moved

We sat together talking of Sally
Ari told me when she had picked up Sal
After leaving me the evening before
Late
Sal had asked her if she hugged me good-bye
Ari told her "Yes"

"Why do you do that?" Sal had asked
"Just like I hug Ken or Keoki
 I hug them like friends"
"But they're married and Zak isn't"
"What difference does that make?" Ari had asked
"Daddy doesn't want you to hug him"

I did not hear what Ari said next
Sal was my buddy
Her protests of our closeness
Dug into me

Riding the fear and pain of rejection

231

I reached out for a moment
Clinging to the immediate future
Of having no plans to look forward too
No meetings or moves or Seminars
When I could see Ari

I felt myself about to step off
Into my garbage
Looked at her
Heard her ask me what I was going through
"Sadness" I said
Then told her what I was feeling
And stepped back into the moment
Her extended hand giving me
The lift needed

She had to leave
For her appointment with Laureen
Possibly to get together afterward
Planning to come back into town
At 5:00
With Sarah for her piano lesson
Our Monday tennis time

She did call
But later than I thought
Too late to meet
Preparing myself for not seeing her
She said she had to hurry to get Sarah
And bring her back to her lesson
"I could come by your apartment"

"Yes!"

We spent an hour
Laying on my new futon
Both tired
Not making love

232

Just holding each other

I told her I was able to see
Sally's conflict
Hearing Mommy and Daddy
Arguing for a month
Aware that Ari and my closeness
Was a problem
Was why I was not around
During this time of trouble with her parents
Easy to see how Sal
Would not want
Her Mommy to do what her Daddy did not like
Actions which she felt
Could only bring pain to her

Ari told me
Of her time with her Mother
The day before
"Your sister tells me you have a friend"
"A friend, yes"
"Your brother tells me you and Robert are fighting"
"It's nothing, Mom"
"Bear it, my daughter"

She told me of her
Treatment with Laureen
Their discussion
Of loving two men at once
"You are ahead of your time"
Laureen had told her
"Take your steps each as they appear
    Take your time"

Ari held me close
Then said
"The only time I feel
    The freedom to be myself

Is with people who are on The Path"

I kissed her forehead softly
"That's what it's all about
    Knowing yourself is the first big step"

I told her how happy I was
She did not call me at night now
She lay in my arms
Not showing any reaction
"As much as I want to hear from you
    I don't want your delicate harmony
    At home
    Broken
    I don't want to risk
    Not being able to see you"
She hugged me
Full and long
"Thank you" she said
Before covering my lips with hers
Kissing me deeply

"Seeing you like this
    It could go on forever" she said
"It might last forever anyway
    But why run the risk" she grinned
Her eyes glistening through her smile
Trying so sincerely to weave
Her two worlds into one

HER SECRET

A day of silence
Passed moment by moment
Living with shadows
Walking through the parking lot
Not understanding why
She did not drive up
Like yesterday

Heart open
Aching
For her love
Which I have
For her presence
Which I miss so sorely

In the evening the phone rings
As I unpack
Filling the corners of my new apartment

Her?
No, Scott
Glad to hear from this good friend
With whom I share
Two unguessable experiences

We both lived part of our childhoods
In Mt. Carmel, Illinois
A town of eight thousand
On the Wabash River
Thick with mosquitos and
Unchanging small town ways
Home of my oldest friend
Nine days older than me

Just before helping with my move
Scott told me of

Streaking his high school in Aurora Colorado
In 1974
With four friends
Of his father's sharp opinion
About the idiots
Who streaked Hinckley High today
Of being busted from school for two days
Happily so
Of his father's enlightenment
Seeing the humor
In his son's act of springtime mayhem

"I knew someone from Aurora
    When I studied sculpture in Greeley" I said
Thinking nothing more
Until Scott asked who?
"Couldn't be the same guy"
I did not remember his last name

The next day I found the name and address
Of Scott's bare-butt comrade
In my old address book
My buddy Paulie
From Greeley
From the art department

Amazing to both of us

Neither Scott nor I noticing
Sculpture
His passion today
My obsession for ten years
Before I wrecked my body and
Had to learn discipline

Happy to hear from Scott
Wanted to hear from Ari

Sinking slowly all evening
Sliding down the wet-mud trail
Knowing it ends at the cliff
Slowing the skid
Staying busy
Putting away kitchen things

Dinner was a drink from a bottle
Of Amino Fuel
Carrot and orange juice
Nothing close to hunger

Ari joked this weekend
About causing two men to lose weight
Thinking about ways to market
Her secret

Ari
With the rich brown eyes
I can see
In my dreams
Driving to work
Now
Drifting so close
Wanting to touch her cheek
Brush her lips with mine

My two-year-old
Squirming
Talons withdrawn
Yet brushing my smooth underbelly
A moment's shift in mood
Away from ripping into me

THAILAND

I awoke in the middle of the night
As though commanded
Unable to get back to sleep
I realized
I was being given a nudge
To record my dream

Thailand was about to erupt
Into civil war
People were being chased
I became one of the chased

To escape
I began moving fast and high
Over buildings
Tall walls and trees
Without regard for gravity
Stronger than I ever remember

I burst out from the area of chaos
Into a serene estate
Pursuers chasing few people
In this forbidden area
Reserved for those in power

Then I dropped from a collapsing roof
Far down
Into a courtyard
Into a group of men
Whom I almost fought

Just before one said
"You're riding The Path"

I awoke

As I remembered the dream
I saw that Thailand
Was Tie Land
Land of my attachments
That I was working hard
On my spiritual path
To free myself from
All that I had created
Which bound me to my human consciousness

Riding The Path

BLUE SUNDAY

Went to bed in a funk
Woke up
Hurting worse

Swam past it
Hoping for peace
Hoping it would not
Take a bite out of my ass

Bigger than my two-year-old
Past life atrocity
Payback
Karmic deep cleaning
I don't know

Usually I know why
I feel what I feel
Choosing to stay with the pain
Or acting out
The question

This time mystery garbage
Piling too deep
To step over
Bogged down in my pain
Must like it
Holding on to it

Saw Ari at Sunday Service
She as low as I
Wondered what I was doing at 2:00 am
"Sleeping"
"You sure?"
"Yes!"

Said she felt I was doing something

Self-destructive

How often do we get nudges
Or dreams
Only to relate them
Specifically
To the events of our lives
Unable to look beyond the many surfaces

I was being self-destructive at 2:00 am
Could not see it then
So had nothing to confirm

What is more destructive
Than hanging on to pain?
Would be interesting to have a greater awareness
Of my inner world adventures
Last night
At 2:00 am

Ari had her own hell last night
Dreams of fleeing the devil
Sagging folds of sadness
Unable to sleep
Terror on the inner
Her brother betraying her
Fear on the outer
For me
For herself

Everything has its price
Opening to Spirit
Not opening to Spirit
Ari is cleansing
On trial by the Negative
Tests come as we take a step
Learning to be a better vehicle
Learning to get out of the way

Letting Spirit do Its will
Through us
Without as much resistance
The Negative challenges
Checking for sincerity
In Its own nasty way

Ari is learning
Is taking steps
Into her lion self
Timidly
So used to pushing down
Her feelings
To please others

She may have more terror
As Spirit cleanses
Each day bringing more strength
Better able to handle the tests
Which get bigger

I nurtured her before Service
Then came up empty myself
Unable to contain my tears
When she decided to not sit beside me
Not to give me that little bit of support

"I don't want people to think we are inseparable"
She said later
"Too late" I said

After leaving the Service as it began
Not wanting to blubber
In front of everyone

Stayed with my pain
With my shit
Did not blame her

Afterward she came to me
Sitting alone in the car
Sorry for what she had done
Open
Loving
But not having enough time
To go for a sandwich

My two-year-old broke through
Jabbing
Crying out for love
Pushing it away
Savagely tired of hurting

We pulled and poked at each other
For as long as needed
To get a sandwich

Healing some before leaving
But still hurting
Her eyes moist
"I wish I could stay with you longer" she said
Off-setting her earlier cry
"I don't know
    If I will ever be able to leave
    The comfort I have with Robert"

The words digging deep into my
Thin skin
Tearing like
Lion's claws on shoji screen

Finding underneath her ten days of
"Things are fine"
Was on-going misery
I had missed

How foolish of me
Knowing
She was the master of facades
Crying out to be herself
Not seeing she had stepped back
Behind her curtain
Even to me
She not wanting to repeat
The same thing
Day after day
"I am scared
    Torn between
    New and old
    Comfort and freedom
    Can't I have both?"

We agreed
I would work harder
Towards seeing her love for me
Whether or not she was able to express it
Whether or not she sat next to me
She would try still more often
To say what she felt

I ask
Sometimes a dozen ways
What she is feeling in the moment

I hope she will not resist so much

She shares
With such beauty
Trembling as the passions
Buffet her
When she dares

When she dares not
She squeezes herself

Into an old corset
Her spiritual constipation
Increasing

As she fills herself with Spirit
Reaching for Soul's freedom
Unrestrainable
And tries to
Hold onto her old consciousness
She walks the walk
Of so many of us
Holding to what is familiar
No matter how painful
Until we get so tired of it
The fear of the unknown
Nothing
Can be as bad
As staying behind
With the same old shit

The makings of Blue Sundays
For both of us

LOST WEEK

Blurring like a bug underfoot
Scurrying for any shelter
I ran from one shadow
To another
Some of them safe
Some crushing down on top of me

Blue Sunday
So long ago
Washed away in brightness
Turning light
For both Ari and me
On Monday

Together during the morning
Unexpectedly
Seventy-five minutes of passion
Before noon

She hurrying home to office work
Probably not to come back into town
For Sarah's piano lesson
And our time together

I back to the office
A good day getting better
Shaking off the funk
Got some work done
Finally
Then she was there again
Unexpectedly
Taking me with her
Shopping
Laughing
Borrowing money
Wallet at home

Driving without her license

A happy quick time together
Sending us both into Tuesday
Not hearing from her
Ok with it
Robert leaving the next day
For ten days
Maybe

Viral haze back again
Just enough to fog me
Ran errands
Chinese doctor
Carrot juice
In and out of the office

Then Wednesday lunch together
Work pushed into the background
In the park
Blankets in my car
And her other car
But not in the Volvo

Bottoms wet from the grass
Staying until she would be late
For her appointment with Laureen
I dropped her off
In and out of the office
To pick her up again in an hour

That evening at home
She called
Not sure our plans
For the next night would work
Not sure her sister
Could take the girls

My cave-in started
Surprised how my expectations changed
With Robert out of town
Not liking myself
Still sliding
Into hurt
Tossed by my two-year-old
Like spoons full of cereal
Onto the floor
Messy
But not blaming her
Staying clear about what I was feeling
Sad
Very sad

The next day
Viral headache
Pounding each second
The morning dribbling by
Garlic every forty minutes
Raw cloves chopped into little pieces
Swallowed like tiny pills
Knowing it would pass
Feeling fear hover
About not getting well
Old fear
Manageable

Ari called in the afternoon
As I lay on my new futon
Caught between distresses
After scrubbing the floor
Because I was bored
Because I could do it and not think
Because I had rested and
Swallowed enough garlic to feel slightly better
Because I don't have much sense

She said we could be together in the evening
No one home to concern her

I shouted with elation
"I bet your headache is gone" she laughed
She was right

I tried to rest
But kept doing things
Then she was there
In my arms
Mine
Yet not quite

After holding her
Asking gently in different ways
She said she missed Robert
My heart dropped
She held me
"I still want to be with you
    I still feel as strongly about you" she said

The pain called seductively
I stepped into it
Wading hip deep
Through familiar muck

Dipping into hopelessness
That her increased comfort with Robert
Would preclude any chance
She and I had
Of being together full time

Hearing her words of love
Unable reach up to them
She held me
As I rode the hard ride
Down and through my garbage

Again staying with my feelings
Not blaming her
Perhaps not being
Overly charitable
As I shared my viewpoint
Hard hurting
Good workout
Maybe I will master
My emotions yet
Choosing neutrality and love
Over pain

We worked through the sadness
Found our harmony again
Let it ripen into joy
Over my first dinner of Korean food
Extra-spicy
To burn out my flu and
Her sniffles

Home to talk and play
Late already
"Dare you stay the night?" I asked
"We'll see" she said
Wanting to pull and rip at her
To will her into staying
I shut-up
Held her
Side-stepped my crap
And slipped smoothly between the sheets
With her
Celebrating midnight
With three hours of love

Neither of us could fall asleep
Knowing she would stay
If I pulled

Knowing it might
Might
Bring havoc into her life
Our life

I did not pull
Supported her in her need
To go home
Called her twice
Before she answered
Just walking in the door

Another hour
Of pain and garbage
Later
We said goodnight
Before the sun caught us

She woke me at 9:00 am
To tell me we could spend the afternoon together
My body numb
Ringing with off-center vibration

Work out of the question
I spent the morning on the phone
Details and birthdays
Wondering if I was still sick
Or only crazy

Met her at 1:45 for a movie
Work paged
Client irate
Hung-up in my ear
Telling me to go to hell
A small miscommunication
I should have caught
Work slipping away

The movie about a Convent
Frantic not funny
Must have been Catholic in a past life
Felt claustrophobic

Pager rescued me
My partner wondering
Why the hell I wasn't in the office
Taking care of this problem

My brain on full fog
Vulnerable in too many ways
I snapped at him
Went back to Ari
So grateful she suggested we leave
Cried in her arms
A few minutes later in the car
Feeling unprotected
Unable to deal with anything

She held me
Not offering unsolicited solutions
Just being with me
Opened to her nurturing
A little

We took lunch back to my apartment
Ignoring the clock
Ignoring her 6:00 o'clock
Pick-up time for the girls

Ate
Made love
Resonated so deeply
Then as I was driving us back to my car
I suddenly turned her car back toward the freeway
Five blocks before reaching my car
Not wanting her to be later

Than she was

A sudden goodbye
As she slipped into the driver's seat
I about to walk to get my car

Which I still regret
Learning later
She had to wait for the girls anyway

Home again
Alone
Loneliness crushing
Outflow blocked
The week a blur

GRIEF

Home again
Nearly midnight
After a morning ride to the North Shore
With Ari
The girls
Their cousins
Gudren and a friend
A morning which stretched into the afternoon
Through dinner
To a movie
And now home

Dropped off like a friend
The subtle pushing away by Sally
Laying in Ari's arms
As I had driven the cousins home
Then myself

Two moments in the day
When Ari and I
Could be together as the lovers we are

Why don't I give up?
Robert
The girls
Hold onto Ari's old consciousness
To wife and mother

Ari's actions say she is not ready
To step away from the family as it is today
To reshape it
To include me
No promise she will ever be ready

Why don't I give up?
Ari's actions say she does not want to live without me

I know I don't want to live without her
So I take these steps
These days
One after the other

Each moment lasting only until the next is ready
Change the only guarantee
Constant never-ending change
Baffling my attempts to maintain balance
Another moment
Another challenge

Tonight
Subtle excruciation
As I look in the bathroom mirror
Grief rising to the surface

Nameless grief
Which suddenly has my father's face
Old dreams
I seem just now to remember
Dreams of not calling him
Dreams of him sitting at his desk
In the bedroom
Copying the parts
From a recent score

Dreams of his grief
His disappointment
At my not calling sooner

Dreams of his face
Red and lined with tears
Eyes shut tight
A death mask
Ending the life of the man I loved
More than my own life

Pappa
Will I ever
Loose this grief
That shadows me
Today
Making hard situations
So much harder

My grief
Echoing with his
Leaving me limp
Lost in my wasteland

Alone
The woman I love
Another man's wife
Her children
Kicking noiselessly at me
"Stay away from my Mommy!"
The cry which breaks through unsaid
Breaking my heart

Can I blame them?
Of course not
Had I been older when
My father brought home his young trombone player
Because he needed a place to stay
Because my father needed a trombone player

Had I been older
When this other man
Became my mother's best friend
Then her lover
Then my step-father
I would have protested wildly
As do Sarah and Sally
In their moments of fear

Instead I was not quite two
Taken with my older sister
To my father's parents
While my mother traveled across the country
With the trombone player
In search of help from her family

While my father quit his job
Grew a beard
Wrote music
Not washing a dish for six months

I was not old enough to protest knowingly
Saving my discontent
For my adult life

CLEANSING

Another night
Tears against my pillow
Ari's sweet voice in my ear
A few hours earlier
Rolling through the morning
On my bed
Instead of Sunday Service
Forgetting to HU
As we promised each other
When leaving the parking lot
Like kids playing hooky

Full moon
Shining on my bed now
Empty
Sunshine gone
The day dwindling after saying good-bye
In the early afternoon

Awakening at 8:00 from a nap
Awakening into darkness
Unable to shake the shadows
Flu not quite gone

Such a wonderful Sunday morning
Running aground
With her leaving

Ari's voice in my ear
Now
On the phone
Waking from her all-evening nap

Unable to come see me
Until when?
Because of the girls

As I teeter
On the cliff edge
Ari says "The more I see you
    The harder it seems for you"

I deny it
Frightened by the possible next step
Of seeing her less
For my own good
When all I can think of
Is seeing her more

"No!
    I'm going through a hard time
    It would be harder without seeing you
    As much as I can"

I do feel vulnerable
Without a foundation
Everywhere I turn
It is difficult
My own making

Seeing Ari opens me
Seeing Ari leave
Each time
Pulls out another
Length of emotional intestine
Rotting
Unusable

The cleansing goes on

SHATTERED DREAMS

Another morning of
Shattered dreams
Tears dripping on the carpet
By my bed

Two nights in a row
Promises to call me back
Unmet

Alone
Crumbling
My two-year-old
Pulling his fetal reflex

Dreading work
Tried throughout the weekend
To pull myself up
To be ready for Monday morning

Now that it's here
All I can think is
"Where's Ari
    She didn't call me back"

My mind knows she fell asleep
Probably with one or both girls

My heart aches
Blinding reason
Spurring the two-year-old

Struggling not to call her
Wanting her to call
Desperately

Wanting her love and support

Wanting to punish her
For leaving me alone

Such an ugly side of myself
When I hurt
Not willing to see
She's doing her best

When happy I see her
Living a challenge of
Love and growth

How can my feelings change
What she does?

Only my two-year-old knows

LOVE RUINED

Only my two-year-old knows
Why it is so important
To hold the pain

Some etched experience
Familiar
Held savagely
Representing love
So hurt a little boy
Unwilling
Unable
To step out of his present
The past

Waving this hurt
In the shower
My two-year-old and I
Conspire
To call Ari
To hear her apology
To beat on her
Like a toy drum
Until the spear-tip of anger is
Removed from my side
Not caring where it lands

Surprise
Worn from feeling my pain
She did not soothe as we talked
As I pulled at her for my comfort
My two-year-old yelled
Tantrum
I watched myself
Throwing words of hurt

At Ari

Ari whom I love
So deeply
I sink to my knees
Thinking about her
Humbled

Ari whose love means more to me than life

Watching as I push at her
Watching as she moves away
Words of anger
Our first angry good-bye

"Maybe you should go back to your family
    Full time"
"Thanks for the advice
    Maybe I will"
"Nice knowing you" I said
Standing in the shower
No water running
Holding the cordless phone
Our words running madly through my mind
Her click
Echoing
Deafening

My two-year-old stood still
His lower lip quivering
"But I'm right"
Frozen in his throat
His treasure
Crumbled in his hand
A deep wail rolling over him
In silence

Then my adult tears

Broke free
Great sobs
Slamming me into the shower wall
Chest heaving
I sank down
Down to the tile floor
Curled into a ball
No water flowing down on me
No energy flowing from me
Love ruined
By my own hand

SKEE BALL

I cried seemingly for days
Pushing away childish thoughts
Of driving off a cliff

An hour later
I called her
Knowing only I must
Own what I did
To not leave it bloody

The children were just leaving
For the pool
She said she would call me back

When the phone finally rang
Ten minutes later
I could hear her anger and hurt
She said she was scared by the depth
Of my hurting
Brought down feeling what I felt

So sobering to hear
Ari say she could not handle
My pain

I know how it felt loving my father
Hurting all the time
Unable
Unwilling
To step out of his pain

I knew then I could not lean on her
So heavily

As was our pattern
After I abused her

With my emotional overflow
I nurtured her
Letting her run through her cycle
Giving her the time to regain her balance

Big of me
How long do I hold onto this garbage?
Dumping on her when I can't handle it

We said good-bye
I told her I loved her
Offered without conditions
Or expectations

Later at worked
Slugging through my backlog
Of ignored responsibilities
I called home to check for messages
Her voice was there
On my machine
Husky from crying
Saying she loved me
Saying she would probably call me that evening
Almost cracking as she spoke the last words

I called her
She sounded clear
She's very good at sounding clear
No matter how she feels
So I knew only that she was past
The worst

We remade plans for dinner that night
With the kids
Korean food

I got a strong inner nudge to go home
Before five

Before I had planned
Before she would be able to call
After dropping Sarah at piano

I waited
Listening to my mind
Moments from finally leaving
She was on the phone
At my house

Kicking myself for not listening to my inner
Wasting twenty minutes
Of the hour we could have been together
I raced to my apartment and
Into her arms

Smiling
Loving
She said if her job was to help me open
So I could process this old pain
She was happy to be of service
No matter how hard it got
She said she was sorry for
Losing her patience with me

I heard her
Felt her
Held her
So grateful
So aware how close I had come
To losing her
Knowing I must do better
Handling my feelings
Knowing it was a warning from Spirit

Sally was with a friend for a couple of days
Ari picked up Sarah from her piano lesson
Returned for me

For an evening of
Korean food
Playful talk of
UFOs
Aliens
Square roots
Mystery stories
How absurd the woman at the next table was
For thinking I was Sarah's father

We walked on the beach
Just missing the sunset
Had long-jumping contests
Rolled in the sand
Then went to the Fun Factory
To blow twenty dollars on fun
A treat for Sarah and me
An opportunity for Ari
To explore her child self
Whom she is touching more often

We watched Sarah play the games
Delighting when she did well
Offering more tokens
For another try
When she did not do so well
We all played Air Hockey
Ari and I playing together
While Sarah cruised the other games
Collecting the tickets for prizes
Dispensed a few or many at a time
From the games

Ari and I watched the woman in black and pink
Playing the Kiddee Skee Ball
So intent
So serious
Planning each shot

For the maximum number of tickets
Like she was at Vegas
Her rent money on the table

I cautioned Ari to be humble
Reminding her that she was watching
The way I watch fat people
When I lose my awareness

Later when I discovered her husband
Tall, rumpled
Shirttail almost out
Lining up his shots
On the alleys of
Adult Skee Ball
With the moves
Of an eccentric pro bowler
Ari cautioned me to be humble
Helping us both to break away with a laugh

Tired and happy
I drove us to my house
To drop myself at home
Feeling the love and harmony
Between the three of us
Cautioning myself
To not get attached
To enjoy the moment
To say good-night with grace

Walking upstairs
I heard Ari's soft words again
As we left the Fun Factory
Suggesting we rent a movie
Go home and watch it
Sarah said nothing
Wanting her mother to herself
I said nothing

So tired
And not wanting to risk the harmony
By staying later with them
Knowing Sarah would feel the intrusion

Hearing Ari's words as her
Coded love song to me
An expression of how she wished
The world could be
For us in that moment

Nothing I wanted more
Except to shed my wants

LOST IN LOVE

Class
Then a two hour Friday night together
Afterward

I drop her home
Concerned she is too late
After playful, tender touching

Robert is out for the evening
Her car in the shop

Moments after walking in the door
She calls
Worried
Robert is not home
An accident?
Following us?

She calls back in half an hour
Still no Robert
Then later another call
More worry

She tells me to get some sleep
I tell her to call her if she needs me
Wanting to hold her
While she hurts
Wanting to hold her
Always

Late in the morning
She calls
A brief moment
To tell me everything is fine

He came home

A little drunk
Staying out
To show her want it feels like

She says she learned a lesson
About considering his feelings
"Are you ok?
 You sound low" she said
"Just worried" I said
Feeling my gut slowly turn
Drowning in the backwash
Of my emotional short-circuit

She lays in my arms
Telling me her love is forever
If not longer
Four hundred years I tell her
When she asks how long I will love her
How long I am prepared to wait for her
I think to myself

Then when her husband is not home
When she could be thankful
He is not there to be angry
That she is late
She worries for him
She learns a lesson
About his feelings

What can this mean to me?
My little self
My little boy
Only that she is moving away

I am not able to comprehend
What she says
That she loves two men

I'm only able to see if she is so worried
About Robert
She cares for him deeply

I'm only able to see if she learns a lesson
About his feelings
Her lessons will come
At the expense of my feelings

Knowing tonight
After the workshop
She now will go straight home
Leaving me
Because of her concern
For his feelings

What the hell am I doing?
My guts are stretched near breaking
Blood red harpoons
Hang from my heart
I am the target on the archery range
Arrows of love
Arrows of pain

She experiences a small corner
Of what Robert has gone through
For months
Straining her

What would happen to her
If I had another relationship
And called her to share my worry
Over the other woman
So obviously
Expressing my love for someone else
She thinks she would handle it
Perhaps she could
I wonder

Could she take what she dishes out?
Would everything blow-up?

Would I lose her?
The only question
meaningful to me

I, who am floundering
A one-woman man
Lost in love
With a two-man woman

LEARN OR DIE

A call to Laureen
To apologize
For being a butt
The last half-hour of class

Gracious
She knew I was doing my best
Yet told me how much
I spread my energy around
Whatever is happening with me
How it affects the class

I shared with her
My pain
Of feeling left out
As Ari shows her concern
For Robert's feelings

Laureen shared her awareness
Gained from her experiences
With Ari and I
Helped me see
Again
My lesson of mastership

Helped me to see again
Needing another to make me feel whole
Will keep me from mastership

"This may be your test
   Maybe the step which takes you
   Above the lower worlds
   It may last many years
   Ari may never be able to put you
   Completely ahead of her husband
   And it will continue to be hard

Until you balance
The male and female within you and
Experience Divine Love"

I sat quietly in my white apartment
Listening to Laureen talk
Feeling her words pour into me
Helping to wash away the film which
Blurred my awareness
Of the nearness
Of the Mahanta
My inner teacher

I sat there
Feeling her love
Feeling my heart opening
Looking at the hard work ahead
Can I do this?
Can I learn to accept the gifts from Ari
For what they are
Learn to enjoy the time we spend together
"You may only get the scraps
    Of a relationship with her" Laureen said

Can I do this work?
Learn this lesson?
Which comes wrapped
In my four hundred year bond
With Ari

How can I do anything else?
Learn or die

THE COMFORT OF PAIN

Driving home from Mililani
Eighteen miles
Halfway across the island
Driving home on a Sunday evening
From an appointment with a client
Driving at an angle
To the violent purple sunset
Throwing off the last orange stronghold
Leaving the sky to night
Moments away

Listening to rock oldies
Something rare
Feeling emotions running through
On their programs
Set in motion by words of love, longing
Heartbreak and teenage boogie

Vision going soft
Blurring
Focusing on road signs only as needed

My attention turns inward
Rising and falling with the swell of the freeway
I feel the music pass through me
Playing my emotions like
The bumpy drum in a music box
Twanging tuned metal fingers

Soon I'm moving against the
Invisible resistance of an
Emotional wind tunnel
Just above the fear that
My pain will resonate with these
Induced feelings and
Dump me into my emotional landfill

Instead I begin to rise through the thickening feelings
Everywhere around me
Able to see them for their illusionary selves
Created only by my consent
Given power only by my choice
Watching the feelings play out
From above

I'm above the feeling
Completely
Having walked up through the clouds
Of Astral sensation
Now looking at the distance between myself
And the mire below

What would I give to maintain this?
A gentle voice whispers through my inner hearing
"Gratitude and discipline will do for starters"

Smiling I see Honolulu's lights ahead
Cherishing the small corner of desire I feel
Deep-running yearning for growth through the pain
Of missing Ari
The pain of being alone
The pain of looking to another
For my sense of wholeness

As much as I wail with pain
The hurting brings a level of comfort
Subtly seductive
Humbling to realize
So hard to shake

TEARS

Against the rocks
Grinding
Forced up against sharp edges
My heart rips with each breath

A day to be together
Made my work last night easy and light
Now a night later
The day strewn behind me
Ruined
Shards imbedded in my most sensitive places

I awoke today with a heaviness
Which had begun at lunch yesterday
With Ari
As she told me of Robert's ongoing involvement
In the new store
For not the first time

The store which was to be hers
Her blank canvas

I overreacted
She was not upset at his role
Only I was

We almost left without eating
But did not
I moved past my discomfort and into
A most enjoyable time

This morning my ignored emotional chills
Were a dull fever
Which I rode alongside
Looking for understanding

Anxious for her call promised at 9:30
To say Robert was off-island for the day
Forty minutes late the phone rang
Two hours later she was in my arms
On my bed
Half dressed

I was wondering what was happening with me
As I held myself back from her
In small ways
Which felt huge when so close to another

She was talking about more things
Shared with Robert

I saw my problem
Too clearly
Just as she asked me what I was feeling

"A little distant from you"
I said as I realized it myself
I felt her shudder
I explained that since
She was growing closer to Robert
I was feeling him more
I explained that she had harmony with us both
My harmony was with her alone
I don't mix well with Robert
I don't want to mix with Robert

He feels too much like my father did
In his insistence that he has no problems
That he has no buried pain
When his childhood traumas
Are so clear in his relationship
With Ari
With the girls
With his business partners

"My relationship is with you" I said
    "You have one with both of us
    Robert and I relate indirectly through you
    But I cannot handle Robert's vibrations
    To feel so much of him
    Pulls me off-center
    That is why I am feeling a little distant"

I did not think too much about her reaction
I was in the moment
Sharing as neutrally as I could

She plunged
Leaped from her happy perch
Down
Down
Down into feelings she had no names for her

As I held her
Coaxed her tears when they would come
Let her turn away for long minutes
Each time to roll her gently back to me
Greeting her return with a kiss and
Soft words

Slowly I learned
She felt her world was crumbling

She loves two men
"Growing closer to Robert
    Does not take me away from you" she said
Unspoken
Was her terror at seeing her love for Robert
Push me away

Or watching me choose to move away

Laying there with her
I wondered if I had set out
Down the path
Leading to our separation
Wondered if I had the strength

It is one matter to move away from someone
When hurting
Staying away is so much more difficult

I asked on the inner
For the strength and clarity
To not jerk her around
With the tantrums of my two-year-old

I knew I was clear and in the moment
Having expressed a feeling
Without blame
Or demand for a solution

Nurturing her
I knew I was in my next step
Giving her unconditional love
To let her heal
To help her open

We spent several eternities
In the next couple hours
She hurting
Curled in ball
Me soothing
Kneading her heart

Finally she opened
Smiling
Loving
Then time leaped ahead again
Threatening our dinner plans

Before Robert's return

She asked me how I felt
"Wonderful" I said
"You turkey" she punched me playfully
    "If you had felt that way earlier
    We wouldn't have gone through so much grief"
Her smile dazzled me as she spoke

We dressed and
I offered to forgo dinner
If it was in her best interest
She said dinner would still work

Ten minutes later
In her car
On the way to dinner
With a quick stop first
At their accountant's just ahead
She said, "Would you mind if we did not have dinner?"
I minded
My distance slipped back in

Waiting in the car
Not able to accompany her
To the accountant's office
Her sister's husband
I battled my feelings
Of being left out
Of anger
Of hurt

If not for the keys in her car
I would have left her a note
And walked back to my car
To sit at the new office
Where painting waited
For my day of play to end

For my afternoon of pain to decompose into evening

She returned
Sensing my mood, she said
"Let's have dinner"
I shook my head
Not wanting her to risk the fragile harmony at home
Not wanting to let go of my pain that easily
Only to have it snap back at me

She drove me to the new office
Plunging once again
Into her wordless grief

We sat in the parking lot
For half as long as dinner would have taken
Her lost in pain and confusion
Me patient but hurting

Soon her pain which I had been feeling all day
Piled upon my grieving
Piled up higher than I could contain
My tears dropped with my heart

She said she could not
At that moment
See the purpose of our relationship
"If you can't see a purpose
    There probably isn't one for you now"
I said feeling overwhelming despair

I softly pleaded with her
To open to her feelings
To give them light

I rubbed the back of her neck
Asking her if I could do anything to help
"There's lots you could do if I would let you" she said

Stunning me

I got out of the car
Walked around to her side
Felt her deep sorrow
Touched her wet cheek
Through the open window
Leaning on her car door

She said she just did not know herself
I ask her to keep trying to learn
"Knowing yourself is the heart of spiritual growth
    The first major step on The Path"

She said, "We'll see"
I heard "Maybe I'll try, maybe I can't go any further"

My tears dripped onto her pants leg
Tears for her pain
Tears for her frustration
Tears for my total defeat
If she stopped trying
To know herself

After she left
I went upstairs to the new office to cry
I cried again in my car and at home

I cried in a blinded walk through the early evening
Through brief talks with Laureen and Colleen

Finally I ate dinner and
Stopped shaking
Then returned to the new office
Painting what I could
At home afterward
I found a message from Ari on my machine

In a choking voice
She apologized for the pain she was causing me
Tried to say something else
Then suddenly was cut off
By my machine
Or her finger
I could not tell

More tears
Two-year-old crocodile tears
Brought to the surface with deep wails

Tears of despair
Tears of being alone
Tears of failure
Tears of knowing the only way through the pain
Was to let her go
To surrender her to Spirit
Surrender to Robert
Surrender our relationship
Surrender the girls
Surrender their marriage
Surrender everything to Spirit

To surrender completely
Then let the joy of being Soul carry me
Through step after step

How the hell do I do it?

ARI WITH ARI

I awoke with two realizations
Laying neatly folded upon my pillow

Opening to her feelings
Opening to herself
Opening to Spirit
Are crucial to Ari's marriage

The soft love
Soft like a baby's crown
This tender, vulnerable love
Ari has developed for Robert
In the past few weeks
Is happening because she is opening
Because she is letting Spirit
Into her life in a new way

Sobered
I saw the primary way
She accepts Spirit's love
Is through me

Will I fail her?
Will I close down
Because I cannot
Handle Robert's energy
Through her

It is so important she sees this
If she cannot find the motivation
To open for herself
She must see that
All she works for with her family
Depends upon her

Then my inner screen flickered and

I saw more deeply into my reaction
Of the past two days
To Ari as
Ari and Robert

The girls left Tuesday at noon
Left for LA and their Auntie
For a week
Before going on to Sweden
For another week with another Auntie
Ari and Robert to join them then
For their family summer trip
Throughout Europe

The girls left after
I spent a wonderful
Monday night with them
Mexican Food
Carnival Carnival
Fun Factory
Home to my house to wait for Ari
To pick them up
My first evening alone with them in months

I was very tired
But when Ari came
My energy overflowed

As we all scrambled across the floor
Playing
Hoarding
Throwing
Pouring fifteen pounds of pennies
Down each other's backs and fronts
Sally said to me "I thought you were tired"
I smiled at her and said "I was"

Later after Sarah bonked her head

On the lanai door
When Sal pushed her off my rowing machine
While Sar lay on the floor
Curled up beside her mother
Holding her head
I bucked Sal off my back
Onto my bed

Laughing Sal said
"Why don't you come to our house and
    Make Daddy laugh"

"That's an idea" I said
Thinking how sad to hear her say that

With the girls gone
Ari who is
Ari with the girls
Ari with Robert
Ari with her parents
Ari with me
So seldom just Ari
Has become Ari with Robert
Only

That he is with her each step
As her store comes together
Without the girls to dilute
Ari with Robert
Is behind my increased awareness of him

My inner screen blinked off
I lay on my futon
Grateful for the morning light
Bumping to a stop
Over rough terrain
Settling into the slush
Of my numbness

Of my dull ache
Of my personal grief
Of my deep concern for Ari
For her to know herself
For her to experience life as
Ari with Ari
Ari with Spirit
Ari as Soul

DETACHMENT OR DEPRESSION?

Has my little boy
Picked-up his bat and ball and
Gone home to pout?

Or have I surrendered Ari?
Leaving my need behind

Have I closed down?
Hurting too much
Drowning in futility
Now Ari is close enough to Robert
For me to feel him strongly

Closed down
Closeting my need
And my two-year-old
Back into the dark

At this moment I feel love for Ari
But no need
Not an overwhelming love
Humbling me with its power
As it has so often
I feel a clear stream of love
Pouring from the center of my heart

Is the flow no longer a torrent
Because
In this moment
I have surrendered my need
And is this stream all that remains?

Or am I feeling the aftermath of
Closing down
Retreating
Surrender or Retreat?

Detachment or Depression?
Neutral or Numb?
I don't know

I awoke from a dream this morning
With Claudia
My good friend and past lover
We were with a group of friends
Watching an erotic film
Claudia and I were in seats
Belonging to people who had not arrived
When the people showed up
I moved to the front row
Claudia chose a seat several rows back
People laughed at us with affection
I turned around
Straining my neck to see Claudia
Ready to act on the impulse to join her

Then I felt she would be resentful
She had chosen her seat intentionally and
Would not like me giving up my choice
Just to be with her

After the movie
A woman who was very familiar to me then but
Unrecognizable now
Came to me
Still in my seat
Still in the crowd
Still apart from Claudia
Offering her affection
With a warm, open heart

I kissed her on her cheek
Then slid onto her lips
With ambiguity
She teased me for my slyness

I felt myself responding to her
Then woke up
With the feeling of being open
To someone new
Of being apart from Claudia
From my lover of that moment

Claudia and I long ago released our attachment for each other
Was this Ari?
If so why did she come as Claudia?

I suspect surrender comes in many herky-jerky steps
I hope this is one of them
I hope I don't screw things up with Ari

My little boy is so difficult to coax
To trust again
After reaching his threshold

Perhaps surrendering him to Spirit
Is my first real step

NO GUARANTEES

There are so many deaths
In one lifetime
So many
I often am not sure
Where one death ends
And another begins

If any part of me died
This weekend
It was a small corner of my attachment

My depression lifted
Saturday
Through several hours and
Two spats with Ari

Sunday began at 9:00 am with Ari
Coming by to pick me up
To spend the morning
Cleaning her new store

For the twelve hours
We stepped from one time segment to the next
After we cleaned
She called Robert
We ran errands and made love
At my old office
She called Robert
We installed a mirror
She called Robert
Circumstance postponed a planned meeting
We arranged shelving and hung paintings
She called Robert
"Since he has helped you so much
    Why don't you take him to dinner" he told Ari
We had dinner at my apartment

Dressed only in shirts
After showering

Made love
Laid in each other's arms
Marveling at the love
Pulsing between us
"I bet you don't know how much
    I love you" she teased
"Tell me"
She thought for a minute
I thought I had called her bluff
"I love you so much it seems odd that I'm married"
I laughed
Hugged her
Told her what a great answer she had
Then said "It doesn't seem odd to me you're married
    Only that you are married to anyone other than me"

She left after we showered again
After a long good-bye
So hard to part
At the end of a day together
So hard to part anytime

So where was my little boy?
Did he come out to play?
Taking another risk
Yes
Perhaps not in quite the same way
He still protects old hurts
In his earnest effort to avoid more pain
Yet he was soothed by my adult
By my surrender to Spirit

I could feel a foundation
Unfelt before
A foundation fragile but buoyant

I felt this support all day today
Felt Ari's love
When she called early this evening
About twenty hours after seeing her last
She showed a different facet
Than when we parted

It had become a pattern
Her going through the changes
Of being with her husband
While I am alone
Remembering her as she left
Then she pops out of a different door
That I wait in front of

I was getting used to it
Slowly
Today was manageable
Hearing her pain
Hearing of Robert's coolness last night and this morning
He told her
She would know if he'd had too much of it
He would leave
She said she cried
I asked her if there was anything I could do
She said "Yes make two of me"
"No problem
    But it will take forty years
    Of being together"
"Guaranteed success?" she asked
"No guarantees
    Only love"
She laughed
I could hear the purr in her voice again
The velvet sound
Which melted me
Like her eyes

Like her lips
Like her touch
Like the words
She gently washes into my ear
After kissing my cheek
At the park

Oh little boy
Come back to play
Come see the Beauty
I've found
Come risk your heart
Come claim your freedom
All you can lose
Is your pain

DISCIPLINE OF LOVE

Some days the bear eats you
This day
This week the bear and I have been friends

A rhythm is building with Ari
She let go of her pain at my slight withdrawal
I slid passed Robert's energy
Accepting her more fully
As she did the same

The love between us keeps me glowing
When I'm not with her
Aware we will part soon
For only seventeen days
Hopefully
For only an eternity
Before meeting in Paris

Working now to stay in the moment
To not mourn my loss
Before it happens

She has been in a mad rush to open her store
I've helped where I could and
Have been very occupied with organizing our new office
Juggling schedules between our company
And Ari

From out of nowhere
Seemingly
I began an exercise
Long known to me
Never practiced
A simple declaration of surrender
Said out loud
When alone

Before singing HU
Or anytime
"I surrender my relationship with Ari
With Robert and the girls
I surrender my business
I surrender my health
I surrender my passions
My desire
My attachment
My anger
My fears
I surrender my life
To God
To Spirit
To the Mahanta"

Saying it out loud
Helps me to hear it clearly

Repeating each day
Keeps surrender echoing
Through my heart

I'm finding a new lightness
Tenuous
But noticeable
Building as I continue the discipline
This discipline of love

SHE'S GONE

She's gone
Leaving tomorrow for Europe
With Robert
To join the girls
Who left two weeks ago
On their own adventure

She's gone
Leaving me with my sorrow
Laying heavy on my heart
A smothering coat of
Bitter honey

Walking gently along a narrow path
Between
The muck and mire of my emotions
And
Stuffing the pain in some recess
Afraid to feel it
Walking this path
Stepping steadily toward
The elusive goal of neutrality

She's gone
Twelve days on the Mediterranean
She said she would say hello
To the pyramids for me

Then a train up the boot of Italy
Through Luzzan
Parting from Robert and the girls
To Paris
To meet me for a week
In Paris

A weekend Seminar

A week of love

Her love lays around my shoulders
Comforting me now
How can this go on?
Two men
One woman
One man dedicated to Spirit
Trying to hang on
Through the upheaval of his human consciousness
The other man dedicated to hanging on
To his consciousness of today
To his pain

She reaching for Spirit
Reaching for the man
Dedicated to Spirit
Hanging on to the man
Who is getting a taste of Spirit

How can it go on?
How can I go on
If it does not?

She's gone
After touching
Which only gets more special each time

She's gone
Yet she lives here
With me
In my heart
Alive and vibrant

LOVERS OF THE HEART

Day Two
Alone like an animal in the woods
Foraging for food
Sniffing the trees
For signs of predators
For signs of Ari

Alone in a world
Rich with work to be done
The company move finished
Settling in now
Eight more days until
I follow Ari
Stopping first in California
To visit my family
Then on to Paris
For a day and a half alone
Before Ari arrives
On Day Seventeen

My guts want to cry out
To run
To seek comfort
"Where are you Beauty?"
My two-year-old opens his mouth to cry
But only warm toddler breath passes his lips

My adult self
Guides him to a warm spot
Sitting together
Holding hands while the pain passes
Smiling
"Yes, this isn't fun
    It also is temporary
    And will pass quicker
    If we sit here quietly

    Watching it go"
My two-year-old struggles
Torn between the pain, reason, and love

Each moment is a step
An opportunity to learn this lesson
To keep growing stronger
Until I can throw off
My lead armor of dependence

Staying at work tonight
Helped to settle me
I can feel a special clarity
Shimmering just ahead
A time when desire is left behind
Mine to create

The stream of moments with Ari
Since we became lovers of the heart
Is a pounding surf of desire
Desire for her
For merging
For being one
For escaping the twisting knife in my gut
By being with her

Reaching for growth
For love

Knowing being one
Can only be done on the inner
Truly realizing myself as Soul
My male and female selves balancing
Blending
Opening to Divine Love

Knowing this principle
Knowing from brief experiences

In the inner worlds of Spirit
From one experience
In the outer worlds of human consciousness

Able to experience
Day to day
So much more
Of this pure love of God
Through Ari
Through loving her
Through being loved by her
Than by myself

Knowing what I feel with Ari
Is the carrot on the stick
The teasing taste of Love

And knowing
For me
This is the way to learn
To experience Love as it comes to me
To let go of my white-knuckle grip
Holding pain so closely
Making each step harder

Will I ever learn this lesson?

Day two without Ari
Trying to become strong enough
To open my heart
To pain and love alike

Reaching for the unfoldment
Which brings a deeper sense of self
Deep enough to flush out my need
Deep enough to free me

EVERY MOMENT

Day Three and I'm in the shit
So lonely
After being clear about
Working to keep my heart open
Working to rise above the desolation
Gathering at my feet
I went out tonight
To the dance clubs
Knowing it could do nothing to help
Guessing I would feel worse
And I do

I did it anyway because I wanted
A whiff of intimate feminine energy
A whiff of illusion
I teased and stoked my desire
Until I could not contain it

Not the end of the world
Not a disaster
A disappointment
As I sit here
Tears beginning to trickle
Stinking of cigarette smoke
My body vibrating out of harmony
As though it had been inside a large brass gong
Rung hard

Pushed away from Spirit
By my own choice
So sad to watch as I take a step backward
Unable to find the strength yet
To walk past this moment
Which I tripped upon

Many hurdles I cleared

This one I did not
Missing Ari so
Missing her love
Missing her voice
Missing her presence
Which I would not be sharing tonight
If she were in town

Yearning for love
Feeling abandoned
Here in this foreign world
This world of pain
Where I must learn to love
Every moment
Before I can leave

FEELING FOOLISH

Dennis
My good friend with whom I shared
The craziness of our twenties
Whom I will see in California
On my way to Paris

I spoke with Dennis today and
learned Linda had been traveling
For three weeks

"I was about to complain
    That I won't see Ari for seventeen days
    But since Linda was away from you longer
    And you survived
    I'd feel foolish to do so"

He thought a moment then said
"Does that mean
    If you don't complain
    You don't feel foolish"

Dennis has a way of finding a unique viewpoint
Often silly
Which I love him for
Sometimes his perspective illuminates dramatically

Feeling foolish for all my complaints
I'm grateful to him
For his words
Which have helped me twice today

Day Four
A slow dance
Through the aftermath of
An emotional mudslide

Work meandered up the morning and
Down the afternoon
In small steps
As I watched the clock
For no particular reason

A confrontation early
Then progress in several areas

Ari hung in the air
As I watched the phone
Thinking of my talks with her
Her breathing in my ear
When I answered the phone
My gut clenching
In hope and fear
Still noticeable but
Now confused

A numb peace lay at my feet
Too worn out to worry
Feeling a small rhythm grow
As the days begin to pile up
Behind me

Tonight I could taste her
As I walked through the mall
Looking at her for hours
In the past
In the future
In Paris
I hope

FEAR'S HAVOC

It is noon tomorrow
Where she is
The day she and her family
Join the cruise ship
For twelve days
When she would say "Hi" to the Pyramids for me

The end of Day Five here
Is the middle of Day Six there
Is she counting too?
Is she missing me like I miss her?
Am I alone dancing through this mudslide?

I hope not
Then see that I am hoping for her pain
What kind of lover am I?

An hour ago a sudden fear
Shattered me
Robert arriving with Ari
At the train station in Paris
Me hiding off to one side
Torn between revealing myself
And returning to the hotel alone
Returning to the Islands alone
To what?
In my inner thoughts, I stepped from the shadows
Said hello
Rode with them back to the hotel
Saw Ari for short visits throughout the weekend seminar
Then flew home a few days early
Desolate

What havoc fear brings

Clearing away the emotional debris

I lay in bed
Reading about a spiritual seeker
Who was forced to watch his wife being murdered

The story puts my pain in perspective
My separation from Ari seems trivial
For a while
Then missing her takes over again
My feelings drift toward open ocean
Swells coming harder
Rudder unattended
I feel so pointless without her

Yearning to wash away
My lost feelings
Instead I plunge deeper into them
Unable to sleep
Unable to find any foothold
To bring myself
Once again to a higher viewpoint

This is the time of growth I know
When struggle goes on
Without relief

If I can surrender my desire for comfort
I may find my next step

OUT OF NOWHERE

Out of nowhere
A blind-side ambush
After a work day
Which refused to jump-start
A simple errand
To Ari's shop
To deliver cotton balls

An innocent introduction
To a naturally seductive woman
A woman who does not try
To be sexy
A woman who shares Ari's birthday
Half an hour talking with this new acquaintance
Who has a boyfriend
Who is a friend of Ari and Robert's
Who did not come on to me

When I left the shop
I was unprepared for
Lightning up my legs
Fire in my loins
The hormonal assault on my brain

An hour's walk on the beach
Only heightened the feeling
I tried to brush back

I almost ran to the courts
Tennis balls loose in my bag
Two people there
On a seven-person practice wall
One of them slim
Asian
Smooth and graceful

I hit the ball better than before
Focusing on the ball
Trying to corral my energy
Yet kept running into her
Moving next to her
Soon I was hitting home runs
Over the top of the wall

Made conversation which
She returned but did not add to
When she left
I was glad to be alone
Before I made more of a fool of myself
Thinking the rampage would soon lessen

Home for a quick shower
En route to the Center for a meeting
Just dried off
A full-length fantasy
Rolled out of my imagination
Snagged my attention and
Went for a sprint
Interrupted only by the meeting
With four women
Who looked to me for spiritual leadership
Two as equals
Two as benevolent trainers

Out of the meeting
The energy rose harder
Coloring my world
With deeper tints of testosterone

To dinner at a health food store
More women
I tried to hide in my newspaper
My radar would not let me

After roaming the store with little to buy
I ran home
Desperate for cover
Not wanting to create any sticky karma
Just before my trip

Fantasies piled up three deep
I locked the door
Rolled on the bed
Finally giving in
Letting my imagination carry me
Love for the single man
Slight satisfaction
Reached for
Hoping it would keep me off the streets

Spent
I lay on my bed
Moonlight spilling in
Through pebbled windows
Unraveling the energy

Shocked at the suddenness
The power to block out reason
Almost
Sobered realizing I had forgotten
The overpowering sexual swings
Before becoming intimate with Ari

Ari
Where is she?
Where is my partner?
With her partner
Her other partner

Laying in the moonlight
Thinking of her
I knew my struggles were with more than passion

Below the sexuality
Lay an urgent need for love
Love I am unable to give myself
Love I closed off to
Love I foolishly look for in others
Trusting her allows me to open
To experience the love we share

Through the jalousie windows designed to let light in
But not neighbor's eyes
The moon hung blurry-edged
Large and round
The full moon
Of course
Not the cause of my surge
But another influence
Not acknowledged

Just as I could not acknowledge
The degree Ari stabilizes me
Without experiencing it

Day Seven
Out of nowhere
Out of no awareness

TO ME FROM ME

Sitting on a Boeing 737-500 on the
Tarmac at Honolulu International Airport
A rudder control module leaking hydraulic fluid

Not to worry
A short contemplation to spur on
The little repairmen of Spirit
To fix this aircraft
If it is the will of Spirit
If it is for the good of the whole
If it is in the best interest of my spiritual unfoldment

Such freedom comes with releasing my concerns to Spirit
When I can

A little haggard but calm on Day Ten
This leg of my trip given a wondrous boost
Two mornings ago
Left for work late
Said hello to my new mailman
Who "Yes!" had finished with my section of the mailboxes

Inside a handful of letters after three days of nothing
Mail comes in bunches now that it is forwarded
Like the comment twenty years ago from
A clerk to a current-day client of mine
In response to her complaint to him
Why a letter had taken five days
To travel the thirteen miles from Honolulu to Kailua
"We wait until we have enough mail to send over the Pali"
A mountain range which costs the government
An extra couple gallons of gasoline every time it is breached

Change comes slowly in government
The forwarding quota reached I sifted through my letters
In back a curious return address peaked out

315

My own
In another's person's hand
I had been looking for a response
From the latest publisher to review my first book
Wondered if they had lost my return envelope and
Addressed another both to me and from me
To be sure it did not come back to them

I opened the envelope
A postcard from Ari!
In an envelope!
I had not expected any word from her
Knowing the delicate balance in her relationship with two men
And the delay from Europe
Would find a letter arriving for me after I had left

The postcard which jumped out at me that day
Also caught Gudren's eye en route to the airport the next day
When she saw my travel document pouch and said
"Can I see it?"
Then picked it up and opened it in one moment
With her youthful innocence

The postcard lay on top
She hesitated
Sensing its personal nature I hoped
Not reading it
Nor recognizing Ari's writing I also hoped
"Can I look at your passport?"
"Sure" I said taking the pouch from her
Relief turned to alarm as she leafed through it
Remembering the only visa stamp to see was from Bali
Evidence of my secret trip with Ari

Before Gudren found the Indonesian imprint
I plucked the blue book from her hand casually and with love

She shared by osmosis

Many unspoken tender times with Ari and me
Keeping a silent knowingness
Often I censor myself wanting to include her in our intimacy
As one of the family

I sat in the plane holding the postcard from Ari which read
"10:45 Hawaii time July 8"
Twenty four hours after I last talked to her
"Just arrived at JFK
   Two hours before another departure for Zurich
   My mind still very occupied with Hawaii
   Wondering how you are
   Wondering what you are doing this moment
   Miss you a lot
   A little more information on my train ride to Paris
   TGV Swiss train leaving Lausanne 5:00 pm
   Arriving Paris around 9:00 pm
   Sometime on my trip to Paris I will try to call you
   Please take best care of yourself
   Looking forward to our Paris time together
   After my long detour it will be heaven
   Many kisses
   Yours Ari"

From her Valentine's Day flowers
I knew "Yours" meant just that and was reserved for me

Such a lift
I felt her lips on mine
Standing in the open area by my mailbox
Underneath the stairs leading up to my apartment
Up to where I last saw her

I admired how she had written so much for me
On a small postcard
Her last line curling around and up

The man with purple dreadlocks sitting in front of me

Pushed back his seat almost into my face
Scrunched in economy class I saw I would not be able to write
Resigned to relaxing
Wanting to write
My body happy for the break
My incessant hunger frustrated

Our delay in taking off lengthened
Annoying the grumpy but gentle man sitting next to me
I closed my eyes and sang HHHHUUUUU silently to calm myself
The flight attendant interrupted me by telling the man
His wife in first-class now had a seat open next to her
"Do you want to join her?"

Waving his upgrade coupons he left me to both seats
Enough room for me and my old laptop to function
Grateful for the gift of freedom
I visualized orange light pouring through me
Relaxing while repairs were made
To the aircraft and my physical body

Once underway I watched the reef runway roll by
Wondering if I would see the group of Hawaiian warriors
Standing beside the runway
As I once did when leaving for the mainland

We left the ground with only ocean below us
The thin veil separating Astral and Physical Worlds
Choosing not to part for me today
Or perhaps the warriors were busy elsewhere

SAN FRANCISCO

Pulled north
Pulled north to San Francisco
I grabbed my laptop and echinacea tincture
Made it past four bellman carts of baggage outside my door
Breaking the trail for a busload of Japanese tourists
Through the lobby and to the rental car below
I drove into Burlingame to get fresh juice
And realized in the store I could not go into the City
Without paying a hard price physically
Probably write crap and
Be in sad shape in Paris

I took my hazy brain
Back to the Holiday Inn Crown Plaza to end Day Thirteen
As I spent the day before
In a thirty-nine dollar room for one-oh-four a night
Staying warm in this brown-rugged room
Quietly watching pay-per-view movies
Resting
Eating garlic
Shooing away the shadows of fear
Fear I will be unable to see Paris with Ari
As she wants to see it
After eleven more hours on a plane
At least I have forgotten to worry about her being there

My body continues its rebellion at life aloft
Sneezing near constantly while aboard the friendly skies
My lungs wheezing heavily for days after
This time the five hour trip to the west coast
Filled my lungs with bubbles the first night here

San Francisco calls
Haunts and memories of that life cry out
The house on 33rd Avenue in the Sunset
Where an old consciousness died

Where my physical body nearly dropped behind me
A gasping shadow holding onto my inner bodies
With the slightest of grips
Not AIDS
Though there were times of ignorant frustration
When I wanted a name for what was wrong with me so badly
I would have almost...

Still no name today
My thirties spent recovering from my twenties
Now I move through my forties building an outer life
Always in jeopardy
As my inner life changes so quickly
Its reflection mirrored in outer circumstance
At risk only because I hold onto my needs
While speeding up spiritually

A baggage door coming unlocked while an airplane taxis
Presents only a minor problem
Should that same door pop open in flight
The plane will shudder violently at best
Break to pieces at worst
I am off the runway
Gaining speed
Not yet at cruising altitude
The baggage of yesterday which only slowed me
Today threatens my very ability to remain in flight
To stay open to Spirit

I screw up my body again
Unable to set aside need
When strong enough to look for fulfillment
In all the wrong places

I do not save money
I do not nurture my physical energy
Beyond being able to get out of bed
When I get it I still spend it

More wisely than before but in the same pattern

Maybe it is best that I did not go to the City tonight
Spirit looks after me in ways I often overlook

I do not need to relive my SF life here
As I'm still struggling to master the old patterns
Which got me into such trouble
Beginning about twenty years ago
When I fell into countless illusionary traps
Looking for freedom

Loving Ari rips away my defenses
Dissolving the jell-coating surrounding old wounds
Which built up during years of recovery
Leaving no doubt about my progress
I cannot pretend to be free of desire
When my desire for her controls every movement and thought
When my anxious neediness controls every movement and thought

Momentary surrender creates vividly calm moments
In an ocean of gnawing fear
Reminding me of the enormity of this step

Can I really learn to love without attachment?
Can I really learn to surrender?

PARIS #1

In Paris
Feeling frustrated with my
Nonexistent language skills

Noon on a sunny Thursday
Day Seventeen
Will she really be at there tonight?
Gare de Lyon is the train station for arrivals from Lausanne
I've been told by both desk clerks

The room is ready for her as soon as I find some roses
I am ready for her
Ready for sunlight
Life without Ari is a shadow existence at best
Which means I am holding on to old pain
Keeping Spirit out

Had dinner with Fatima last night
A flight attendant with United
Whom I met on the plane coming here
Liked her energy
Liked the music in her voice
An Algerian living in London
Who likes to answer questions with "Guess"

I guessed
The continent she lived on
Third try
But not Algeria
The month she was born
Second try
Her name
After she gave me two of the six letters
Her birthday on the third guess and
Her birth year dead on with my first try

Fun playing with her on the plane
Lots of sexual attraction
Wondered what I was going to do about it in the evening
Caught as I was monogamous with a woman who was not

I don't want to be intimate with anyone but Ari
I also don't handle alone time very well
Kicking away little thoughts of Ari and Robert
Of their intimacy
Of her choosing to be with him
Not me
My mind easily makes me crazy
As it did in the middle of the night

After dinner and laughter with Fatima
And the conscious decision to not become physical
I collapsed into the bed
Thirty-six hours and six thousand miles after getting up
I awoke at what should have been dawn
But I think it was closer to midnight
Very dark very quiet
In a room which could almost be
The small desperate room I had in the
El Capitan in the Mission District of San Francisco
Where I spent a desolate week eight years ago
Between La Posada crisis center and Baker House
Because the mental health system in SF was overflowing
My body falling apart then
My emotions billowing in downward directions

I awoke in room fifty-seven of the Hotel Acacias Etoile
In Paris
Much different than the Mission in San Francisco
Except in the middle of the night
Shadows suffocating as I lay soaked in sweat
Wondering if she would come as planned
Or would she call to say she could not
Her marriage on the line

Or one of the girls sick

Or would she show up with Robert
Unable to come alone
What would I do with both of them here in Paris
Tag along as a menage a trois?
My emotional body preferring suicide

Would she be there to tell me
She could not see me after this week
That Robert had given her another ultimatum
Or that she had had a change of heart
That Paris would be like Bali
Opening our hearts
Only to have them cut out at the end of the week

Or would she
Would she
Would she
My mind gained strength from the darkness
HUing did not help
Perhaps because I have been singing HU little on this trip
The spiritual worlds open up with discipline
With determination
Finally I laid back in the arms of Zand, the Mahanta
Feeling the wrap-around cushion of His Love
I surrendered to Spirit and asked for Zand's help
Asking over and over
Finally I fell asleep again
Leaving the thoughts of despair with the night

PARIS #2

When I think of her I see her softness
I see the gentleness in her eyes
I see the muted tones of her clothes
Designer colors made for a tasteful funeral
She shuns brighter colors
Feeling more at home with the subdued

I can feel the touch of her cheek against mine
As I wait in the Gare de Lyon
Hoping her train is on time
Desperately hoping she is on it

21:17 the woman in the information booth had written for me
When I asked her in English
What time the train from Lausanne arrived
After she had said "Je ne parle pas Anglaise"
And scribbled 21:17 - C on a scrap of paper
Pushing it through the window
I presumed the C meant which platform and
On platform C I waited as a train pulled in at about 9:15

People began spilling off
Just as I noticed a second and a third exit stair
Half running one direction then the other
I was suddenly worried she would not see me and
Slip away down the exit I was not watching

Caught in my dance
Bouncing from shoulder to bag as people swarmed around me
Holding tight to a single red rose
I saw her walking towards me
Carrying one bag
Pulling another behind her
Wearing a moss-green checked shirt and pants
Which I remembered the girls teasing her about
"It looks like pajamas" Sally had said

I loved her in the loose outfit

She stood in front of me before I could run to her
Smiling her smile of Beauty
Drowning my heart in happiness
I held the rose out to her before either of us spoke
Then she was in my arms
Heart to heart
Her body pressed hard into mine
Her hair against my cheek for a moment of shyness
Then her lips melting me from the inside out

"Hi Beauty"
"My love"

We stood on the platform with time suspended
Then finally left
Hurrying for the taxi to take us to the hotel
As our bodies began forming into one

"How's the hotel?" she asked
"Humble"
"Oh? I thought it was a three-star"
"More like a half"
We laughed and snuggled into the back of the taxi
"The lift fell this morning with three people inside"
"No! Were they hurt?"
"Well yes
 They are all in the hospital"
"Maybe we should change hotels"
"My sense is that it will be OK
 Besides I don't think there are any empty rooms
 Remember the Tour de France?"
"Of course" she said "It will work out"
I held her grateful neither of us had been on the elevator
Then said
"The people must be working through some heavy karma
 To come to a Seminar and fall five stories in an elevator"

"They are on The Path?"
"Oui"
"Oh my" she said then snuggled even closer
"My bilingual love"

The weekend blurred as we spent much of our time in bed
Loving, touching, laughing, spilling massage oil
Spilling our hearts all over each other
We attended part of the Seminar
Arriving late for the Friday evening session
Barely making Saturday afternoon at all
But there just in time for the Sunday Morning HU Song

We saw a few people we knew
But talked little with anyone
Having our own Seminar For Two

I was so tired and still slowed down by my lung infection
During two workshops on Saturday I felt a surging heat
Then my body seemed to be struggling
With the initial stages of an oppressive new illness
If the onset of the flu is being steam rolled
Then I was being crushed under a falling mountain
Worried that I might collapse while still with Ari
I surrendered any and everything to Spirit
Going with the moment
Whatever it might bring

The sun was out Sunday afternoon after the Seminar ended
We returned to the hotel to prepare
For an afternoon by the Seine
Ari wanted to read in a park by the river
An old yearning of hers without a present-life connection
After a walk through the sun and
Crowds awaiting the ending of the Tour de France
We crossed the Seine
But found no grassy areas along its banks

Just beyond a busy street stretched a promenade
Scattered with people enjoying the Sunday Sun
Leading to what we later learned to be the Musee de Armee

We settled in the middle of one section
Ari spread her Sarong on the ground and
We stripped down to our swimming suits
Or red silk boxer shorts in my case
The pair with the button on the fly

For three hours we laid by, on and over each other
Like affectionate puppies
Watching Americans Brits Swedes Germans
Play soccer football frisbee
Two French fellows won the day's artiste de frisbee
Without contest
Spinning kicking cursing laughing at each other
One had a high-pitched voice, mutton chops and
The mannerisms of a clown
His friend laughed like Mozart impersonating a hyaena
And laughed mostly when the squeaky-voiced clown
Dropped the frisbee

Ari read parts of a rough draft of this book
I read Tom Clancy's newest
And we soared with the sun
Our love
And the precious time together
My body healed in moments it seemed

Monday and Tuesday we drove the maid crazy
By barely getting out of bed and leaving our room
Before she ended her workday
We searched for Indian and Mexican food
Found them
Then gave up trying to match our tastes
To Parisian food
We visited the Louvre on Monday

328

Interesting but not sensational
Monday evening we took a late, short nap
Then went to the Crazy Horse for the last show

The girls were stunning
The numbers interesting but too similar
Subdued erotica
I loved sharing it with Ari
She at first seeing only women being used as sex objects
Then found the beauty in their bodies and movements
And by the end of the show she had brushed slightly
The tingle of stimulation

I was surprised when she said
The show would have been more erotic
If the women had not always worn
The tiny stringless G-strings

It was fun to share the world of erotica with Ari
Sharing it in a balanced way
I was elated my energy stayed in my heart
Did not lock into my loins
Knowing that I have a problem
From over-indulging in titillation
Knowing that erotica
As an occasional seasoning is fine and healthy

On Tuesday we traveled to Versailles
Enjoying our limited mastery of the Metro
Agreeing we both liked the buildings
Better than what they held
The Grand Canal and the grounds were wonderful
We got off the little tour tram at the restrooms
On the way back and discovered rowboats for rent

The next couple of hours were a side trip to heaven
Me rowing clumsily
Ari laughing at me while reading aloud parts of this work

"Pretend it is someone else's writing
 Pretend you have never heard it before"
She told me when I expressed my doubt
At hearing my words aloud
So she read to me
I love to hear her voice
Reading talking singing
It does not matter
She read to me and I liked what I heard
Surprise
Did not mean that anyone else will like this piece
But I did and she seemed to, which was enough

She read
I rowed the length and width of the Grand Canal
A wondrous private lake for Louie the whatever
To soothe his troubles

The day before after our Crazy Horse adventure
After another night of more loving than sleep
I had suggested she wear a skirt and experience life in Paris
Sans panties
She thought it sounded like great fun
But at the last moment
Over my mocked-up protests
She slipped on her "security"

Tired of rowing we let the boat drift
In the back arm of the canal
Where no other rowers ventured
I slid down into the bottom of the boat
Hugged her legs and laid my head on her lap
As the boat swayed on the small waves
As she read
I ran my hands up her skirt
Caressing her thighs
She moaned slightly but kept reading

Moving my hands up farther I found her waistband
"What are you doing rascal" she said
"Raise up a moment"
To my surprise she did and I whisked off her panties
"Give them back" she demanded smiling
I promised I would but did not say when
Relaxing back against the rowing seat
I put her panties on my head like a cap
And enjoyed completely the little glimpses between her legs
Her wrap-around skirt could not prevent

She pretended to be scandalized
I took pictures of her with my disposable camera
"What are you shooting" she wanted to know
As I arranged and rearranged her skirt
By the end of our photo sessions
She was playfully hiking her skirt
Mocking the girls of the Crazy Horse

The launch came to tell us we must return
The park was closing
She rowed back a little way
Then my male side kicked-in and I took over
Rowing her back to the dock
Taking my queen back to her palace No woman has ever deserved
a man's love and playful affection
More than Ari

My love for her grows passed where long ago
I thought I could not love her more

PARIS #3

Walking back through the Park at Versailles
Now almost free from the afternoon hordes of tourists
Other tourists
We held hands and talked softly, glowing
I asked if she would like to go to the Pigalle area
Where the hotel staff had told us the hotter shows were
Hotter than the Crazy Horse
She said "No" and not a lot else

I was disappointed
Wanting to find a Crazy Horse sans G-strings
Wanting her to want to also
Hoping Parisian nudes would be more interesting
Than the porno pandering in the rest of the world

Perhaps my little boy stamped his feet and I missed it
Perhaps I reacted to Ari's discomfiture
At my history with strip shows
She expressed pointedly

The most wonderful afternoon of our Parisian holiday
Dissolved into a heated argument about values
About her involvement with fine food and materialism
About my inability to solve my passions
"You give up so easily" she said
Referring to me going again to a Honolulu dance bar
After she expressed her upset
Which she learned by reading the manuscript
And saved until now to throw on the table

We ranted on
She well seated in her suppression
I waving my anger around the grounds of Versailles
Like some flag of a personal nationality
I attacked her inability or unwillingness
To open her feelings

A terrible thing to do to someone just learning
To trust herself and her lover
To trust my sincere interest in her feelings

She attacked my disappointing behavior
I reached deeply trying to show her
What I struggled with
Why I was doing the best I could do
That I too wanted to lick my urge to run from my pain
But that I had tried suppression and
It did not work for me
I was trying to work with energy as it ran through me
Trying to go with my natural flow
Trying to guide it instead of block it
Showing more compassion for myself

As we left the dirty beige rocky parking lot
In front of the Palace de Versailles
We both let go of our upset
She seeing my inner workings more clearly
I regaining my compassion for her
Detaching from my anger
I apologized for being a jerk again
She forgave me
And we headed back to our half-star hotel
For our last night together in Paris
Both grateful it was not like our last night in Bali
When we thought we would never spend another night together

On the Metro she said
"I'll go with you tonight to the shows on Pigalle
    So you won't have to go without me
    Tomorrow night after I leave"
"Only if you are really comfortable" I said
"It would be good for me
    To learn more about how a man thinks and feels"

PARIS #4

"I don't like the way he smells
   He stills eats a lot of meat and
   His breath smells like rotten flesh"
Stunned I held her
"I love him more than I did during—
   A while ago
   Much more
   But it is still not very good
   We don't really talk much
   We spend a lot of time together
   But we never talk about feelings and issues
   With the honesty and detail you and I do
   He talks about so many things
   I just don't care about anymore"

I had asked her how often she and Robert spent time together
As closely as she and I had spent the past six days
She opened up
Showing me the reality behind her assurances that
"Everything is OK with Robert"
I had heard for the past six weeks
She had told me the first night in Paris
He had said our relationship did not bother him anymore
Amazing I thought
An attitude I would fall short of myself

I know how readily feelings defy reason
How one moment a situation is totally acceptable
The next it is worse than death

"Our sex life is awful
   He doesn't want to kiss
   So we don't
   He doesn't seem to need that kind of intimacy
   He doesn't like oral sex
   So we don't do that

Oh he has discovered he can make me cum
By going down on me
So he does that
But not very often
In twelve days on the ship
He spent about ten minutes being intimate
In the two weeks leading up to that
We made love one other time"

I held her as she poured out
Feeling closer to her than ever
Trying to brush aside the hope that
She would be with me full time in the future

"He confessed he has had
    Emotional and sexual problems in the past
    He goes through a constant struggle with you and I
    Trying to give me room to have the experiences
    He knows I have missed
    And he continues to come out with his cutting criticism
    Of any and everything
    It's just awful most of the time"

We held each other so tightly it seemed I was the one talking

"He was so loving when he put me on the train to come here
    Yet I am worried
    There will be a terrible backlash when I return"
"I wish you did not have to go back" I said
"I hate it that I have to"

We made love with Eastern Forest scented massage oil
Slipping between our bellies
We bet a trip to Tahiti
On who was the closest to knowing what time it was
In the middle of the night
I lost and
Declared that since I now had to pay for our trip to Tahiti

335

I got to say when we went
"You did not include that in the bet" she teased
    You need to think a little farther ahead next time"
She laughed and tickled me in our ongoing dance
To protect her family unity
To win her for myself

At dinner earlier she had asked me
Where I would wear a wedding ring if I got married
Knowing I wear no jewelry
Except a Carnelian necklace
For its possible healing properties
"Maybe around my neck
    Or if it was not metallic on my finger
    Where would you like me to where it?" I asked
"Ask your bride"
"Maybe I am"
My words jolted her noticeably
Even though I have asked her to marry me many times
Now
In the future
Anytime anywhere
She flushed and held my hand
Our silence filled to overflowing with a love
Which continues to amaze and confound me

Later as dinner ended and we decided to forget Pigalle
She said
"I would like to take back everything I said today
    About your life when I am not around
    Go to Pigalle
    Don't go to Pigalle
    Do whatever you need to do
    I don't want to get in your way"

Feeling her love
Feeling her desire for my freedom
Hoping she will someday want her own freedom enough

For us to be together
I said "You are my way"

PARIS #5

Wednesday we did outstay our maid
She knocked
Then left towels at the door
With a laughing burst of French neither of us understood

When finally out of the hotel
We took the Metro to Gare L'est
So Ari could purchase her ticket
For that night's train ride back to Switzerland
Back to Robert and the girls
Back to her other husband
She had been as vague to me when she arrived
In explaining why she had to leave Wednesday
Instead of Thursday
As she was in finding out which train to take back

The ticket seller could not tell her
Which train met her needs
But he did tell her
That her expired Eurail pass
Could not be extended for a small fee
As she had been told on the train to Paris

With no longer any possibility
Of her using the Eurail pass
Which I had understood to be the main reason
She could fly out Thursday morning
Giving us another night together
While putting her back in her family's arms
At about the same time

I asked her once again about flying
She said "no"
I pressed
She said "It would not be convenient"
My little boy

Already rattling his crib to get out
Went ballistic
"Well I sure as hell would not want to INCONVENIENCE you"
I hissed at her and stormed off
I did not go far
Being away from her was not the desired effect
A lesson learned long ago
I did want to be away from the maddened child in my guts
Wielding his crimson torture instrument of the day
Searing my very tender heart and underbelly

When in this state I am at my most miserable
Because I know I am making my life wretched
While doing the same to someone I love
In this case Ari

As she waited in the information line
To learn which ticket to tell the ticket seller she wanted
I looked ominously at the reservation desk
Hoping it would not join in the absurdities of the
Cumbersome process of buying a single ticket

Standing around uselessly
Not wanting to do anything to help her leave me
I bitched and moaned
Escalating into near viciousness
Reviewing the faults of her marriage
In an unkind way

When she told me Robert was to meet the first train
Thursday morning
At the station across the road from his father's house
I understood why she needed to go back by train

Undaunted my two-year-old kept up his little head of steam
I began attacking her lack of forthrightness
When I asked her the first evening
About why she had to go back early

She stabbed back with little jabs
But was mostly silent while I raved
When she finally had her ticket
And we were outside in the sunshine
I calmed down
But ten minutes later at a cafe
I set off again on my pillage of discomfort

She nearly left me there
Feeling so overstuffed with my garbage
With her own unexpressed feelings of frustration and hurt

I almost yelled at her to yell at me
To let out her feelings
When she finally did let a short jet of anger escape
I cheered her on and we both laughed

Somehow, we got through that time
Finding our way across the city
To dinner
Healing and reviewing our worst fight in not long enough

Ari makes-up after a fight
With tenderness I don't feel I deserve
Since I am usually the only one upset
But we did make up in time to split Pesto and a pizza
In time to snuggle for thirty minutes in the hotel
Before she frantically packed and
We raced to the Metro
Through eleven stops on the Vincennes line
And six more on the Bobigny-Picasso line
Until we arrived at Gare L'est
Nearly late for a train we suddenly could not find

French train stations are not set up
For people who cannot read the language
We found it with eight minutes to spare

Almost running
Me sweating heavily
Having said little on the dash from the hotel
Both silently with our pain

She hurting to leave me
Thinking about how her family will receive her
About how she will be able to continue balancing
Her life with two husbands

Me feeling like I am running a gauntlet
Peppered with debris
Carrying a long sword out in front of me
Sharp end pointed toward my belly
Waiting for the inevitable fall
Waiting for the inevitable running through

Why does it have to be this way?
Why cannot I go my way gracefully
With sadness
With whatever I feel
Why do I have to come apart like a toy soldier
Stepping on a too real land mine?

We stood on the train steps
She holding me tightly
Not happy she had a cramped berth with several young men
"Let's figure out exact travel plans first next time
 We could have gotten you first-class last Friday"
My little boy still wanting someone or something to blame
Ari agreed and we held onto each other
As tightly as we could
My little devil tried to kick up resentment
That she did not seem to hurt as much as I
I quieted him quickly
Too absurd an accusation when my complaint of the day
Was that she did not show enough of her feelings

The whistle blew and I got off the train
Catching a quick last kiss
I watched her pull away
Hurting as though I would never see again
Tears running free
I finally turned away unable to see her anymore
Falling predictably on my sword

Hugging myself as I walked back along
The incredibly empty platform
So alone in this City of Light
Slowly turning to a City of Stone for me

Her name
Her face
Her touch everywhere I looked
In everyone I saw
Every step we had taken arm in arm
Throughout this magic city
Now haunted me
Feeling more alone than I could remember
I did the one thing which felt familiar

I headed for the unexplored area of Pigalle
The word "Pig" shouting out at me from each sign
Pointing the way to my destination

The Metro was hot
The evening was hot
Paris has summer days which seem
To begin at noon and last until ten or later

I surfaced finally
After a ride of only a few stops which took lifetimes
Into a garish world of neon and swirling crowds
Two different pitch men outside strip bars
Overstepped my sense of acceptable persuasion
At nearly the same time

After yelling "No" to the first
I ripped my arm away from the second

Ari laughed in my ear
She hovered nearby asking me why I needed to do this
I suddenly saw her in her train alone
My heart ripping in two at her loneliness

I passed through more crowds
Finally going into two clubs
Only to return to the sidewalk without sitting down
The shows were awful
Explicit
Without imagination or grace
I found a third club I could set in for one mineral water
While a very bored woman disrobed with a silly expression
Then left the stage to its emptiness
I explained to the two women
Suddenly sitting on either side of me
That I was here to sit alone not to buy them drinks
When they looked hurt
I told them I had just put my lover on the train and
I needed to be alone
They left me then
I left moments later to be asked by two men out front
If I wanted to see a live sex show
If I wanted a girl for the night
At both my "Nos" they acted mystified
What kind of creature could I be?

So grateful Ari had not been with me
That I had not subjected her to Pigalle's crudeness
I caught the Metro back to the hotel
Facing the room which had been such a palace for us
Looking out the window by the bed
Overlooking the courtyard
And the window of the 102-year-old woman
Living in the building next door

Ari had seen her opening the shutters the first morning

I had seen her finally that evening
When we returned to the room after dinner
We watched as she closed her blinds
"As slowly as she opened them the other day" Ari said
"I like her a lot"
Now the old woman's shutters were closed

I packed hoping the morning would come quickly
Then crawled into bed
Curling up into a fetal position

When the morning did come
I bathed and finished packing
Looked at the courtyard one more time
Saw that the old lady's shutters were still closed
Wished her good health from both Ari and me
Then dragged my bags
Down six floors of tight and twisting stairwell
The lift not repaired

Through the flurry of a long taxi ride
Airport security
Check-in
Customs
Not knowing which gate
Then finding it
I ached for Ari

Finally on the plane
Lucky to find an empty seat next to mine
So that I can maneuver the old laptop
Too large to use in economy with only one seat
I promised myself to write my two battery's worth of power
Before my energy faded
For I did not write a word while I was with Ari
Just like Bali

Too consumed with being her to think about writing

How I would love to spend enough time with her
To be able to break away and write
Without feeling I am losing time with her
Irreplaceable time together
An hour too large a proportion of our available time together

How I would love to spend time with her
Ongoing
This woman whom I love and need
More than anything I can imagine

I felt pushed back in my seat as the plane took off
I leaving Paris about the time she arrives in Switzerland
Both facing another week apart
Perhaps longer if she stops in Los Angeles
To restock her store

HOME

My Dearest Ari
How can I begin to apologize?
How can I go back and change our last day together in Paris?

You asked me in the middle of my anger
 "Please don't send me off with this burden"

I responded without mercy
Without regard for harmony
Saying I would not stuff down my discomfort
Just so you could leave happy and light
Then continued with my tirade

I feel we can communicate better
But can I do much worse than to self-fuel my hurt
By lashing out at you about our inadequacies?
I think not

I am grateful Spirit gave us an opening of laughter
Grateful we took it
So grateful we did not part in anger.

You have had a day and half with your family by now
I hope you have washed away
Any lingering bruise from that time

I have not
It is hard to heal one bruise
Self-inflicted or not
When another blow lands in the same area

The fine line of scar tissue
Not healed by the time we said good-bye
Lingers near the edge of my heart
Reminding me that I was pig-headed
That I dumped garbage on the last hours of our honeymoon

As we called it with such love and tenderness on Sunday

I am so sorry
I wish I could take it back
Wish I could have said to you
"It hurts me so for you to leave
    Hurts so much that any little effort
    Left undone
    Which could give us another minute together
    Seems unacceptable
    Seems unbearable"
I wish I had said that
Instead of all the crap I did say

Our time together is so precious
You are so precious
I can just barely bear to be away from you
Just

The flight home was a long long journey away from you
A journey of survival
For I could not stay in Paris without you

Yet now that I am home
I find this is not home anymore
This new white apartment of mine is no longer home
Honolulu is no longer home
Hawaii is no longer home

I have no home
Except when I am with you

Our time together in Paris
Stands alone in my heart as my home
Missed desperately
After having grown so close to you

I can only live with the lingering scar tissue of my anger

Knowing I caused it
Knowing I do not want to cause more
Hoping I do not
But I probably will
Pig-headed as I can be

I love you beyond words
More than imaginable I wish you were here with me

THE RAWEST OF DETERMINATION

Only my relationship with Spirit comes before Ari in my life
My little self protests even as I write this
That "NO!" Ari comes first
Spirit second

Luckily I am aware of experiencing
The principle of being able to love another
Only as much as I love myself
Loving me begins with giving
Giving my efforts to Spirit
To be the best vehicle for It
I can possibly be
To do Its will

I watched my father block his heart
To anything but his wishes
I felt him hold onto those he loved
Suffocating himself
Dragging down those around him
In the name of love

In my love for Ari I walk a fine line
Between giving to her and
Pulling from her the energy my two-year-old demands
The neediness of my little self requires so much attention
I spend most of my energy in my relationship with Ari
Even when she is not with me

I am holding onto pain old and new
Staying tied to the dock
Wondering why the next step is coming so hard

There is a time for nurturing
A time to stand still holding myself
As I heal
As I learn about love

349

This time is passing
Standing still is about to turn into stagnation
Decay will soon follow

I sense it in my relationship with Ari
If I am to win her
If I am to win my freedom
I must choose it with each moment

"You give up so easily" Ari said
She was right
In some ways I do give up so easily
My focus is splattered
It is wonderful to drop everything to be with her
In the few moments of freedom she can find
It has become unavoidable to moon over her after she leaves
This holding on to the memory
Of our last time together in the physical
Is beginning to numb me
Is blocking my ability to be with her in the inner
When not together in the physical

I sense doorways nearby
Doorways I have longed to walk through
Doorways I do not want to miss again

So with the rawest of determination
I step onto this next turn of my path

Twelve hours after leaving the plane from Paris
I was at work
Not expected until after the weekend
Our company is vibrant and challenging for me
An opportunity to be of service to people in foreclosure
An opportunity to earn a living for myself
To clean my own cage

To travel with Ari I need to reach a new level of income
To reverse today's slow slide into debt
To declare to myself that I can be successful
Not just getting by
A bright but hampered person
Doing as well as can be expected

The business is there
My training and experience are sound
I need only to focus
And work my butt off

I have floundered through three years of writing
Some periods moving well
Others stuck fast in my mire of confusion

Whenever I hit my stride
When I breathe the rarified air of creating
For long enough to feel the inner rhythms take over
Knowing I am astride and have only to ride
I jump off
Time and again I feel high and invulnerable then
Take this energy out and away from writing
Into some lower chakra pursuit
And lose it like pouring liquid gold down the sewer
Needing only more determination to break the cycle

I have more help today than I have ever dreamed of
Spirit waits by my side as always
But now I hear
Now I know
Now I have only to choose to listen

Ari's love is there to balance me
I must take responsibility for my neediness
It is not her job to heal me

At the Seminar in Paris

During a short exercise in a workshop
I saw Ari and me in a past life
Two men working together as one
I then chose anger and destroyed the balance
Ending the time together
My job today with Ari is to re-establish the lost harmony
To heal my own pain through opening to Spirit
To help her grow into her own freedom
Without condition

Our situation prevents merging in the physical
Yet I am so open loving her
Open as never before
Giving Spirit the window through my defenses
To flow in and heal
My job is only to be a good patient

So it time to focus
Time to finish this book
Time to give my full efforts to work
Time to prove to myself than I am worthy
Worthy of Ari's love
Worthy of Spirit's patience
Prove my worthiness by choosing to fill each moment
With my very best efforts

About the Author

BC embraces life's adventures by focusing more on what he is doing than what he has. Relying on spiritual awareness, often called intuition, helps him to see the hidden lessons behind everyday encounters. Learning (still!) that ignoring this inner guidance often makes the road rougher to travel, he accepts opportunities to unfold however they come.

When asked about his writing, he explains, *"Forty years ago, I found I had little to write about. Ten years later, I began to develop my writer's voice."* Today BC lives in Honolulu with his lovely wife Sweetie, delving into his personal experiences and imagination through his writing.